'Watson's Flaxborough begins to take on the solidity
of Bennett's Five Towns, with murder, murky past
and much acidic comment added.'
H. R. F. Keating

Blue Murder

'You've seen the film, have you, sir?'

'I admit to that dubious privilege.'

'Is there anything about it to which you feel you should
draw my attention?'

The barrister reflected briefly before replying. 'No – that
is what I find somewhat perplexing, and my clients have
been unable to clarify the issue. You see, those sections
of the film involving local people are perfectly innocuous records of public occasions. The sound-track,
as I am led to understand, is itself indecent, but of
course it has been added later. So have certain all-too-
explicit displays of concupiscence by anonymous – indeed, unidentifiable – performers.'

'You say that the pornographic parts of the film are not
contributed by local people, but how can you be sure if
those taking part are not identifiable?'

Heckington frowned deeply. He clearly did not care to
be on the receiving end of cross-examination.

'Too professional, my dear man. Altogether too
professional.'

The Flaxborough Novels

'Whatever's Been Going On At Mumblesby?'*
One Man's Meat*
The Naked Nuns*
Broomsticks Over Flaxborough*
The Flaxborough Crab*
Charity Ends At Home*
Lonelyheart 4122*
Hopjoy Was Here*
Bump in the Night*
Coffin Scarcely Used*
Plaster Sinners*

*also available in Methuen Paperbacks

COLIN WATSON

BLUE MURDER

A Flaxborough Novel

A Methuen Paperback

A Methuen Paperback

BLUE MURDER

British Library Cataloguing in Publication Data

Watson, Colin, 1920–1983
  Blue murder.—(The Flaxborough novels)
  I. Title II. Series
  823'.914[F]   PR6073.A86

  ISBN 0-413-40460-9

First published in Great Britain 1979
by Eyre Methuen Ltd
This edition published 1987
and reprinted 1988
by Methuen London Ltd
11 New Fetter Lane, London EC4P 4EE
Copyright © Colin Watson 1979

Printed and bound in Great Britain
by Richard Clay Ltd, Bungay, Suffolk

For Anne

Chapter One

FRIDAY WAS MARKET DAY IN FLAXBOROUGH. IT WAS A somewhat tenuous survival, perhaps, but not yet an anachronism. Long departed, certainly, were the little wheeled huts – not unlike Victorian bathing machines – in which corn and seed chandlers shook samples from small canvas bags into the palms of farmers, each the size of a malt shovel, and invited them to 'give it a nose', whereupon the farmer would inaugurate the long and infinitely casual process of making a deal by observing unrancorously that he'd seen better wheat dug out of middens. Nor were animals any longer part of the market-day scene. The iron-railed pens and corridors; the weighbridge; the show ring, pooled with the pungent staling of bullocks and stained here and there with dried-off urine that looked like lemonade powder; the raised, half-round, open pavilion with a clock tower on top, where the auctioneers impassively interpreted twitches, nods and glances from the stone-faced butchers and dealers: all these had disappeared from the Market Place. So, too, had the drovers, those wondrously misshapen but agile men, who hopped, loped and darted among the sweating beasts and intimidated them with wrathful cries and stick-waving. In the long, black coats, roped around the middle, that they wore in all conditions of weather, the drovers of Flaxborough had looked like demented medieval clerics, bent on Benedictine and buggery.

The market-day crowds now were indistinguishable from those on any other day – or in any other town, for that matter. Not for many years had there existed the sharp contrast between townsmen and countrymen, expressed chiefly in the visitors' dogged affectation of blue serge, brown boots, and a hank of sun-bleached hair, spittle-slicked over a brow the colour of new brick. These – the 'country johnnies', as they had been termed contemptuously by the girls of Flaxborough High School – had long since adopted the conformity of casualness in both dress and grooming, and were safely anonymous.

Yet Flaxborough Market flourished in its modified form and continued by virtue of a four-centuries-old charter to defy the rationalizing zeal of county and national government.

One Friday in early August, Police Constable Basil Cowdrey was strolling slowly past a row of stalls where home-cured bacon and hams, sausages and other vestiges of a cottage food industry were still to be bought. It was a good part of the market in which to encourage, by slow and diligent passage and re-passage, kindly thoughts concerning a policeman's lot (to say nothing of respect for his powers of discernment in matters relevant to the Food and Drugs Acts) and Constable Cowdrey was prepared to be pleasantly surprised sooner or later by the deliverance into his custody of a pound of sausage, plump, meaty and well saged and peppered in the style of Moldham and Gosby Vale.

His first tour was unproductive. This did not disturb him. He went on past the vegetable sellers and stood for a while staring at a man who sheared lengths of dress material with an expression of pained reluctance upon his sweaty pugilist's face.

The man grew aware of Constable Cowdrey's presence. His shears were stilled and he moved his gaze just far enough to meet the policeman's eye.

'Want something, son?'

The nostrils of Constable Cowdrey paled and twitched. Unhurriedly, he moved to the side of the stall, ducked his helmet to avoid the canvas awning, and loomed beside the sad-eyed proprietor like an army of occupation.

From this vantage-point, he contemplated the four or five women who were waiting to be served. He spoke quietly but with grave deliberation.

'Do there exist upon these premises suitable means for the washing of hands as required under the terms of the Borough by-laws relating to market trading and the control of slaughter-houses?'

The women looked at one another, then at the bolts of cloth, the stallholder, and the policeman once more. Two of them shook their heads vaguely.

The trader sighed. The shears resumed their partition of dress lengths. 'Van,' he said.

'Van?' The quite superfluous mention of slaughterhouses in

his own question recurred to Mr Cowdrey's mind and confused him. He had been thinking too hard about sausages perhaps. Was this fellow going to try and make him look silly? 'Van?' he repeated.

'That's what I said, son.' The head of the cloth salesman gave an impatient, indicative jerk. PC Cowdrey looked behind him. At five or six yards' distance, parked close to the West Row corner, was an elderly green Bedford. One rear door was open, trailing half a yard of pink material.

'That's not premises,' the policeman said.

The salesman began parcelling a folded cloth length in a sheet of newspaper. 'Not a slaughterhouse, neither,' he remarked to the woman nearest him. The woman glanced at PC Cowdrey and tittered.

Emboldened by this show of disrespect, two of the customers embarked on a spirited debate – ostensibly between themselves, but accompanied by so many meaningful glances at everyone within hearing that public oratory seemed their real purpose. Under discussion was the foolishness of authority in general and that of PC Cowdrey in particular.

'Washing hands is for food. Stands to sense. Comestibles. That's food. Comestibles. Them [a wave at some rolls of tweed] isn't bloody food, duck. *He* [a contemptuous finger pointed at Mr Cowdrey] doesn't eat that uniform when he goes home to dinner. He's got mixed up. He's bloody smock-raffled. Don't you [direct and stern regard upon the salesman] let yourself get pushed around, duck. He's on about comestibles. Food. [To the world at large.] That's right, isn't it?'

PC Cowdrey knew that nothing weakens the force of law more surely and rapidly than irresponsible attempts to involve its representatives in what his sergeant termed 'argy-bargy'. He turned upon his heel and stepped out at once towards the van, which, 'premises' or no, he was confident would contain no more suitable means for the washing of hands than a wet flannel stuffed into an old biscuit tin.

It was an unfortunate moment for such decisiveness.

Into the narrow strip of the Market Place between stalls and pavement, from which wheeled traffic was excluded on a Friday, there had entered a vehicle of such imposing proportions that no one thought to challenge its progress through a prohibited area. This strengthened the delusion of the driver that he had chanced luckily upon some sort of clearway or by-pass, so he accelerated in order to take full advantage of it.

For a fraction of a second, PC Cowdrey's brain marvelled at the message it was receiving from the far extremity of his optic nerve. Seemingly so close that he might lean upon it and mist with admiring breath its fawn-coloured coachwork, great crystal lamp glasses, and a radiator like a silver temple, was a Rolls Royce motor car.

Then admiration was transmuted into athletics. In one co-ordinated movement, PC Cowdrey made a ninety-degree reverse spin, simultaneously toppling back in the manner of a felled tree until his body was at the correct elevation and pointing in the right direction for his ready-primed leg muscles to propel him to safety. He leaped from the path of the Rolls like an ibis and, to the great wonder and approbation of the ladies who so recently had derided him, landed square in the middle of the wares of the cloth sales-man, whose stall (or premises) collapsed and forthwith immured the policeman in a welter of canvas, spars and unfurling rolls of cloth.

The car did not stop, but in the quiet isolation of its interior the incident was remarked upon by the three men and a woman who occupied it.

The driver said: 'Stupid sod!'

His companion in the front passenger seat, who had a pale, no longer young, yet healthy face, with a touch of saintliness in its good looks which might have proclaimed a successful faith healer, said: 'I don't think it was very clever of you, Robert, to flush that particular bird. It had a helmet on, old boy.'

'Only to begin with,' observed the man behind them after making a rearward review. 'He seems to be wearing a very loose turban at the moment.'

The girl also had been looking through the back window. She leaned forward and grabbed the shoulder of the saintly one. Her face was urgent, ecstatic. 'Christ, Clive! He was! He bloody was! Ye village bobby, no less. Bob's slain the bobby, darling!'

'Nobody's slain anyone,' the man she had called Clive said sharply. 'Stop being a silly cow.'

The girl looked more delighted than ever. 'It'll be shittikins for Robert in the village lockup tonight. Hey, Bob – you know what they do to their felons in these parts? I mean, for Christ's sake, they geld them just for nicking turnips!'

So stark was her make-up that even while she grinned, her eyes continued to look like two big bullet holes.

Clive half-turned. 'Birdie, my dear, your high humour is a great tonic at the right time, but just at the moment it bores my tits off. OK? This, old girl, is not a village. It is a town and doubtless possesses more than one policeman. We are not yet out of it – and from the way dear Robert is driving at the moment I'd be surprised if we ever do get out of it. So keep the funnies until he gets his nerve back.'

Birdie's companion on the back seat made for her a grimace of wry commiseration. She shrugged and began to suck her little finger.

The Rolls was travelling more slowly now. It reached the eastern end of the Market Place and continued in a direct line into Corn Exchange. At the end was a T-junction. 'Left,' said Clive.

The driver obeyed, swinging the car into the narrow culvert of Pipeclay Lane that led to East Street and escape.

Or it would have done, had not Sergeant William Malley, coroner's officer, stalled the engine of his ancient and much abused car a few minutes previously. It lay now, a stranded black grampus, athwart Pipeclay Lane, with Bill Malley standing alongside and staring with calm compassion at its flanks.

Clive stiffened and grasped the driver's arm. 'Christ! Road blocks already. They've actually set up bloody road blocks. I don't believe it.'

Birdie giggled nervously. 'Oh, shittikins,' she murmured.

The driver felt for reverse gear. Clive shook his head. 'Just stay put, old boy. Act thick. Me London idiot, no compree. OK? Let me do the talking.'

Sergeant Malley looked up. His eyes widened and he removed his cap in order to run plump fingers through the cropped scrub of his hair, but nothing extreme in the way of surprise overtook him. Had it been Nelson's flagship that had just rounded the corner, he would have shown but the mildest curiosity.

Birdie was still bent upon harrowing her companions. 'He

doesn't need a bloody car, that one,' she said. 'He's a road block all on his own. Look out, Bob, he's coming to squeeze you to death.'

The sergeant was indeed approaching and his girth was undeniably impressive. The driver groped uncertainly for a button and the window beside him glided soundlessly out of sight. There appeared in the space a couple of Mr Malley's chins, then, as he stooped, the rest of his large, regretful, amiable countenance.

'Sorry about this, sir. I've sent for a bit of help. I shouldn't think it would be worth your while to try and back out.' He glanced back towards the Corn Exchange junction and shook his head before inserting it within the car and blandly examining the furnishings.

Clive had been craning forward in his seat in order to intercept whatever stern questions the policeman might address to Robert. He now decided to take command before his increasingly apprehensive companion did something else in the button-touching line and committed fenestral decapitation.

Clive smiled so that when he spoke some of the smile seeped into the words. 'Oh, come now, officer – there was hardly call for you to summon reinforcements. We have no intention of becoming fugitives, I assure you – my colleague here least of all.' He bent the smile a fraction to indicate Robert.

Malley, long accustomed to the obtuse humour of coroners and lawyers, offered no comment. He simply nodded and snorted gently once or twice like a somnolent bull. Only the girl was perceptive enough to recognize that he had no idea what Clive was talking about. She gleefully kept the knowledge to herself.

'We couldn't stop before, actually,' remarked Clive. 'Not without causing an obstruction. So my colleague here' (a soft 'Jesus wept!' in the back compartment) 'decided to drive into a side street and wait.'

'Oh, aye?' said Malley. He had not been listening. There was a lot of Birdie's leg displayed in the tasteful setting of the blue-grey upholstery of the rear seat. Clive interpreted the vagueness of his acknowledgment as cynicism. He did not feel happy.

Suddenly the bray of a siren reached them.

Malley withdrew his head and straightened. He peered towards his own car, then turned and looked in the opposite direction.

He gave a shrug of disgust. 'The twats!'

Much puzzled, the car's occupants looked first at one another, then back through the rear window. A patrol car, its roof lantern flashing, it seemed to them, with unwontedly furious intensity, was drawing to a halt close behind.

The sergeant made a God-help-us face and said to the patrol car driver as he emerged: 'Trust you to come to the wrong end of the lane. Now all you've done is block this gentleman in. My car's . . .'

'Never mind your car, Bill,' interjected the other patrolman. 'This is the lot we're after.' He jutted his chin nastily in the direction of the Rolls.

'Why? What are they supposed to have done?'

'You'll have to ask Baz Cowdrey about that. It was him radioed in, just as we were leaving to move your heap.'

There was a gentle clunk, like the closing of a bullion vault. Clive stood by the door of the Rolls and asked if he might be of any assistance, gentlemen.

Patrolman Brevitt, the one with the expressive chin, whose air of pugnacious energy was emphasized by a cap pulled very low over his eyes, replied: 'All in good time, sir.' The innocent phrase sounded like a threat. Brevitt's special misfortune – or talent, perhaps – was a manner of address that in his mouth would have transformed even Tiny Tim's 'God bless us, every one' into a demand with menaces.

'Here's Baz now,' said the patrol-car driver, a much more benevolent character named Fairclough, who treated his colleague as a delinquent younger brother in need of good influence.

Constable Basil Cowdrey paused at the lane end and surveyed the scene of ambush with grim satisfaction. He said something brief to his left shoulder, from which an antenna had lately sprouted, then set forth. Clive noted with some alarm that the radio aerial was not the only fresh feature of PC Cowdrey; he had also acquired an heroic limp.

Fairclough felt he ought to say something to ease the tension. 'That officer,' he explained to Clive, 'is the complainant, we understand. That means he's going to accuse you of something. Or your driver, rather. But he'll ask questions first, of course. We were just sort of asked to make you available, if you see what I mean.'

Brevitt, who had been listening, drew back his upper lip to

expose big yellow teeth. Clive was put in mind of an angry horse.

Cowdrey arrived. His antenna had been retracted, but not his limp. Canting heavily upon what appeared to be a permanently shortened leg, he unbuttoned a pocket and drew out a notebook, then – rather pointlessly, everyone else thought – laboriously buttoned the pocket up again.

He freed the notebook from its lashing of black elastic and produced a short pencil which he examined for some moments before deciding which end to put to use.

At last, he looked at Clive. 'You the driver of this vehicle, sir?'

Clive blessed him with a smile of forgiveness. 'No, no, officer, not I . . . but perhaps I should make introductions. My name is Clive Grail, as you may or may not know. The lady in the rear seat is Miss Birdie Clemenceaux, my research assistant.' He indicated the driver. 'My photographer, Mr Robert Becket. Anyone else? . . . Ah, yes, Mr Kenneth Lanching, there in the back. Colleague, you know. Same stable.'

Strictly a non-metaphor man, the constable looked sharply and with new suspicion at the travellers. 'Oh, it's horse-racing you're connected with, is it?'

'Oh, Christikins!' trilled Miss Clemenceaux, her head thrown back. Lanching turned aside and grinned. Only Robert Becket showed no amusement but continued to stare blankly at the knob of the gear lever.

'Journalism,' explained Mr Grail, 'actually.' He again smiled kindly, as upon a penitent who was still a bit confused about the distinction between worldly and spiritual. 'Investigative journalism. *Sunday Herald*. Need I say more? Grail is my name.'

'Yes. You said.' The constable limped to the opposite side of the car and stooped. He also winced very obviously. Clive hastened after him and addressed Becket.

'Come on, Bob: the officer's having to bend down to talk to you.'

Becket gave a start, then clambered from his seat and stood beside Cowdrey.

'May I see your driving licence, sir?' The question was put with that classic casualness which implies that failure to comply with so reasonable a request there and then will be construed by any judge and jury in the realm as admission of intent to deceive.

'I'm afraid it's at home,' said Becket.

Deep in the interior of the Rolls, Miss Clemenceaux murmured something to Lanching and both laughed. Grail glanced in at them crossly.

'Your certificate of insurance, then, please, sir?'

'Home,' Becket said.

For a long moment, Cowdrey studied the author of this defiance. He saw a stocky figure in a suit with rather a lot of pin-stripe in it. One hand, square and thick-fingered, was held loosely at waist level in an attitude suggestive of habitual coin-tossing. The head, disproportionately large, had close-cropped patchily greying hair. Becket's moustache, too, was closely trimmed – an exact rectangle of stubble across the width of his upper lip. Ears were small and chubby, as was the nose. The restless, slightly inflamed eyes were deeply set above plump cheeks, which they irrigated from time to time with a tear.

None of which features registered upon the consciousness of Constable Cowdrey. His scrutiny was intended not to gather impressions but to make one. When he judged that enough time had elapsed for this purpose, he directed his attention to the open notebook, flexed his pencil hand, and prepared to conduct the catechism proper.

'Your name and your home address, if you please, sir?'

Sergeant Malley, by now bored almost to the point of exas-peration, made a low-voiced representation of his own. 'You'll not be wanting the lads any more, will you, Baz? I mean, I'm still stuck there outside Haywards and his fish van can't get out.'

Without interrupting his chronicle of Mr Becket's habitat, function and itinerary – a process so slow that Birdie said it was like being in bloody Egypt and waiting for an inscription on your bloody tomb – the constable nodded solemnly and Malley shooed the patrolmen into their car with instructions to back round and get busy with a tow rope.

The small crowd of market-day bystanders, who had congre-gated in hopes of there having been a bank robbery, gradually dispersed, but only after making the disappointing discovery that a backing police car does not sound its siren with notes in the reverse order.

Clive Grail made one or two further attempts to interpose sweet reasonableness between the coldly persistent policeman and an increasingly resentful Becket, but they seemed only to be making matters worse. He retreated into the Rolls and sat, looking very thoughtful, between his colleagues on the back seat.

'I've got a growing feeling,' he said softly, 'that this little town is more than commonly afflicted with bloody-mindedness. Take a look in *Willing's*, there's a good girl, and get the address of the local paper.'

Miss Clemenceaux opened a compartment in the bulkhead before her. It proved to be a small reference library and stationery store. She picked out a book and thumbed through pages.

'Ah, very sturdy-sounding, darling,' she said. 'The *Flaxborough Citizen*, no less. In Market Street. It probably organizes lynch mobs.' She giggled. 'Poor bloody Robert!'

'Never mind Robert. Who's the editor?'

The girl again found her place in the guide. Her frown of concentration suddenly gave place to a delighted grin.

. 'Goddikins! Better and better. Josiah Kebble, would you believe? *Josiah!*'

Chapter Two

MR HARCOURT CHUBB, CHIEF CONSTABLE OF FLAX-BOROUGH, was as nearly an agitated man as he ever allowed himself to be in any situation other than one concerning his greenhouse or his home-bred Yorkshire terriers.

'What on earth, Mr Purbright,' he exclaimed, 'was the wretched man thinking of? Actually to arrest the fellow.'

Detective Inspector Purbright regarded Mr Chubb with an expression of tender concern.

'I really don't know, sir. I'm only sorry that it isn't a matter that comes within the province of the CID.'

The chief constable was only too well aware that this was true. It added to his annoyance at having chosen so lamentably ill-timed a moment to 'pop in', as he expressed it to Mrs Chubb, 'and see how things are' at the Fen Street police headquarters. Market days were generally safe. But now the impossible Cowdrey had ruined the record.

'Of course, you realize that there isn't a magistrate to be found in the town,' said Mr Chubb gloomily.

Purbright knew that he was going to be asked a favour. He recognized the off-hand, tendentious way in which the chief constable tried to disguise a sense of dependence upon the good offices of an inferior.

'Yes, sir, I do see what you mean. The special market-day licensing hours. Pubs open all day.'

'That is not what I meant, Mr Purbright. Really, you make the members of the bench sound like a lot of dipsomaniacs.'

'Have you . . .' Purbright paused and appeared to be thinking very hard. 'Have you tried Mrs Popplewell?'

'She's on holiday.'

'Ah.' Another pause, then, 'What about old Austin Kelsey, sir? He doesn't need to stay in that shop of his all the time now that he's re-married, and he can manage to keep sensible just about long enough for a quick remand job.'

Mr Chubb's ill-ease deepened. He had an abiding dislike for irreverent phraseology. A 'quick remand job' indeed. It was not the inspector's style to be flippant – not in his, the chief constable's hearing – and this present lapse could only mean that Purbright was enjoying the situation and intended to exacerbate it if he could.

'No, no.' The chief constable shook his head and prepared to accept a petitioner's role with as much dignity as he could preserve. 'Kelsey's hopeless, poor old chap, as we all know. And this business could prove delicate. There are journalists involved – London journalists of some standing, I understand – and they can be very tricky fellows.'

'They can, indeed, sir,' confirmed Purbright.

'The trouble is, Mr Purbright, that the affair got rather out of hand. Cowdrey was upset – understandably – and formed the view that it was a case not of careless – nor even of dangerous – driving, but of deliberately attacking an officer in uniform. He arrested the man and told him before witnesses that he would be charged. Very serious, you know.'

'Very.'

Mr Chubb reflected unhappily that his inspector was never more anxious to echo his opinion than at those moments when he ardently desired the reassurance of a rebuttal.

'Naturally, I had no choice but to back up my own officer. I don't like it, but there you are.'

Purbright shrugged and smiled a melancholy, fatalistic smile. Mr Chubb looked away.

'There will have to be a special court, so we shall have to find a magistrate,' he went on. 'I don't mind looking after things, of course, but your preliminary assistance . . . you know – actually locating a JP . . . I mean, that really would be appreciated.'

Involuntarily, Purbright gave a little half-gape of surprise. The chief constable had never, in the many years of their association, made so abject a plea.

'Well, I can't promise anything, sir, but I'll certainly have a word with my sergeant and see what we can do.' At the door, Purbright glanced back. 'The gentleman in question – Mr Cowdrey's alleged assailant – he's in the cells, I suppose?'

By this final provocation, Mr Chubb's sorely-tried composure was very nearly broken. 'No, he is not,' he said sharply. 'As a matter of fact, he struck me as being a fairly personable sort of chap. I'm having him wait in that little room at the end that Policewoman Bellweather uses sometimes.'

'Ah,' said the inspector, in the extravagantly understanding manner wherewith collusion in crime is acknowledged by one hopeful of a cut of the proceeds.

As the door closed, Mr Chubb drew slow breaths and tried to think of the world as a great Cruft's. It was a long time before even this image began to yield its customary comfort.

By mid-afternoon, evidence of the exciting events in the Market Place had disappeared. The cloth salesman's stall had been re-erected, his scattered wares collected, brushed down, and put back more or less tidily on display. The constable had not, however, returned. The woman at the home produce stall whose turn it had been to render tribute unto Cowdrey glanced from time to time at the small parcel she had prepared and wondered if she should accept one of the more optimistic rumours (which ranged from the policeman's suspension from the Force to his actual demise) and let the contents go to some money-paying customer.

Four o'clock sounded from the great tower of St Lawrence's church. The stream of shoppers had thinned and now flowed more sluggishly between the rows of stalls.

A short, shiny-cheeked man in rimless spectacles strolled across the south-eastern corner of the square and entered a shop in whose window was a group of choice antique furniture pieces, some cut crystal and a cased pair of eighteenth-century dress swords.

He was Barrington Hoole, optician, of Chalmsbury town, and he clearly was expected by the proprietor, who announced, without preamble: 'They're here.'

Mr Hoole pressed his lips together and made a high humming noise at the back of his nose, at the same time nodding like a spring-loaded Buddha. It was his way, apparently, of expressing gratification.

The shopkeeper, a stooped, sandy-haired man, with deep facial furrows and scraggy neck, went to a cabinet at the rear of the shop. He selected a key from the fob pocket of his aged but still elegant grey suit and opened the cabinet, the doors of which were glazed with tiny panes discreetly reinforced with steel lattice-work. There was something ceremonial about the performance, not unlike the reverence with which the senior partner in a wine-shipping firm might draw from sanctuary a very rare brandy.

It was not a bottle that was lifted into the waiting hands of Mr Hoole, though, but a rectangular, leather-covered case, about a foot long and three inches deep.

Mr Hoole carried it to a glass-topped table nearer the light. Carefully, he set it down and unhasped the lid. He drew a clean handkerchief from his breast pocket and rubbed upon it his plump but delicately tapered fingers.

The antiquarian (for thus Mr Enoch Cartwright described his latter-day metamorphosis from junk dealer) watched in silence as the lid of the case rose. Then he glanced at Mr Hoole's face and smiled at what he saw there.

'Oh, yes,' said Mr Hoole. 'Ah. Yes, indeed. Mmm. Yes.' He wrinkled his small, beaky nose, and sniffed happily.

'Rather nice?' prompted Mr Cartwright.

The optician hummed and raised an eyebrow. He shrugged and

hummed again, this time in a speculative kind of way; enthusiasm did not do when price-naming was imminent.

'You notice the crest, of course.' From Mr Cartwright.

'The loony earl. Ye . . . es . . .' Mr Hoole was smiling gently, as at some fading but still fragrant memory.

He eased from its bed of scarlet velvet one of the pair of pistols that the case contained. 'A trifle on the heavy side,' he said, snuffing the smile lest it warm any expectations.

'Lovely balance,' countered Mr Cartwright at once.

'Funny how many of these old horse pistols are still around,' mused Mr Hoole. He peered dubiously at the weapon's stock, as if a fissure had suddenly been disclosed. 'And some of them in very fair condition.' 'Like those, for instance.' There was nothing wrong with Mr Cartwright's reflexes.

Mr Hoole puffed his cheeks, said nothing. He picked up the second pistol and cradled it in both hands. With its bell-shaped muzzle, it looked more like an antiquated motor horn than a firearm.

There came the sound of the shop door opening. Both men looked round.

They saw what appeared to be a youth of about twenty, eager-faced yet diffident in manner. He was dressed in sports jacket and trousers. His first concern, it seemed, was a medieval Japanese war helmet hanging just inside the doorway, but on hearing the proprietor's approach he abruptly and a little guiltily switched his attention from that fascinating article to Enoch Cartwright.

'Good afternoon, sergeant,' said Mr Cartwright.

Detective Sergeant Sidney Love, who was a good deal older than twenty and sometimes wished that he looked it, nodded cheerfully.

'Inspector Purbright's compliments, and could you spare him half an hour,' he said, then added reassuringly: 'Just a remand. You know. In and out. No bother.'

'What – now?'

The sergeant shrugged good-naturedly. 'Well, you know . . . when it suits you . . . within the next ten minutes or so.'

Mr Cartwright, who did not look very pleased (but knew, unlike Mr Chubb, that the delicacy of his dual role of magistrate and dealer in sometimes dubious properties placed him under certain special obligations) said that he would be ready as soon as he had dealt with his present customer.

'Good-o,' said Love.

He strolled across to see what the little bloke in rimless specs was looking at.

'Nice duelling pistols,' he remarked, after some moments' silent admiration.

Mr Cartwright gave a short, mirthless laugh. 'Duelling pistols,' he echoed. 'Hardly suitable for duels, sergeant. Not bell-mouths. Ha ha. Oh, no.' There had crept into his way of speaking an academic drawl that friends of the former occupant of a Broad Street scrap yard would have found decidedly odd. It was what Purbright called 'Enoch's JP voice'.

Love glanced at Mr Hoole, as if seeking reprieve from disappointment.

The optician seemed to have been using the time he had been on his own to cultivate a downright contempt for the goods on offer. He responded to Love's appeal with a disparaging pout and 'No, he's right, of course. Just a couple of common horse pistols. Provenance unknown.'

Mr Cartwright glared at this imputation of illegitimacy. 'They're Purdy's!' he declared. 'Not a doubt of it. Hand-chased for the seventh Earl of Flaxborough. Superb examples.'

Mr Hoole bestowed upon the sergeant a sad, knowing smile. 'Purdy's!' With one fastidious finger, he flipped shut the lid of the case. 'Dear me!'

There were further exchanges of a similar kind. Love told himself that these two nuts might be at it all afternoon and evening if he didn't do something about it. He looked at his watch very ostentatiously, as might a boy at a new birthday present.

Mr Hoole eventually thrust the case under his arm. 'I shall come back,' he said to Mr Cartwright, 'when you are in less demand by the constabulary.' Halfway to the door, he turned. 'Don't worry about these; I'll look after them.' A pause, then, 'Such as they are.'

'Quite a character, your friend,' remarked Love, as the shop door closed again.

Mr Cartwright, JP, glowered. 'And tight as arseholes,' he replied. This time his voice sounded perfectly natural.

The occasional court was held in one of the ground floor rooms at Fen Street police headquarters. A certain informality was conferred upon the proceedings by the sparsity of the furniture – two folding chairs and a card table – and the presence, in various corners, of a stolen spare wheel, a stack of back numbers of *Horse and Hound*, and a tea urn awaiting repair.

The chairs were occupied by Mr Cartwright and the young woman on loan from a nearby solicitors' office who acted as deputy clerk of the court. Between them was the small table.

Standing close by – so close, indeed, that he seemed to have been placed to umpire some projected hand of cards – was the prisoner, Robert Becket, 38, photographer, of Ardrossan Court, Paddington, London.

Even the chief constable, gamely occupying the role of prosecutor, was obliged by lack of floor area to share in the general intimacy. He stood, papers in hand, almost shoulder to shoulder with Mr Becket, to whom, on one occasion, he actually offered apology for knocking his elbow.

As for the prisoner's colleagues, only one – Clive Grail – had managed to squeeze into the room at all. He was wedged between the pile of magazines and PC Cowdrey, who gave evidence of arrest. Birdie Clemenceaux and Lanching had to be content to stand outside in the corridor.

Fortunately for all concerned, the chief constable took less than five minutes to catalogue Becket's alleged misdeeds, request an adjournment until the following Thursday, and observe that the police offered no objection to bail, which he suggested might suitably be set at five hundred pounds.

'You will be remanded,' said Mr Cartwright, with enormous solemnity, 'for six days, and granted bail in your own recognizances. Do you understand what that means?'

'Do you?' countered the defendant.

The chief constable intervened. He made to the magistrate a slight bow, more dismissive than respectful, informed Mr Becket that that would be all, then ushered him, in a bustling but quite amiable manner, from the court.

Chapter Three

FRIDAY BEING PUBLICATION DAY AND A NATURAL BREATH-ING space between one week's news-gathering and the next, there was no need for Mr Josiah Kebble to be present at all in the tall, ramshackle building in Market Street that housed the editorial offices of the *Flaxborough Citizen*. His appointment as editor, how-ever, was a recent one, having followed upon certain unfortunate events in the family of George Lintz, the previous incumbent, and he had not yet assessed how sharp an eye was being kept upon him by his distant but voracious employers in London. So he had come in. The better to display his diligence, Mr Kebble had moved a desk from the office used by Lintz – a remote and private room on the upper floor – down to the open area behind the counter. There he sat, in view of the double glass doors leading from the street, a sort of benevolent monarch, ready (and, indeed, eager) to grant audience to any member of the public, with the exceptions of a Miss Cadbury, doggy charity organizer, Bernadette Croll, the Mumblesby nymphomaniac, and a very sinister-looking barber called Tozer, who was more than likely to upset the two office girls, Sylvie and Carole, by ogling them fiercely and asking them if they had ever considered entering the lucrative and interesting profession of housekeeper.

On this late Friday afternoon, the editor was entertaining a visitor from the neighbouring town, whose newspaper, the *Chalmsbury Chronicle*, had been Mr Kebble's charge until recently.

The two men were giving Cartwright's pistols close scrutiny, Mr Kebble with the aid of a jeweller's glass that he had taken from one of the multitudinous pockets in his gingery tweed waistcoat.

He looked up, plucked out the glass, stretched his face once or twice, then pushed a pair of heavy-framed spectacles to the bridge of his button nose. 'Aye,' he said, 'they look all right, Barry. Who knocked them off for him, I wonder?'

Hoole was sitting side-saddle on the edge of the desk. 'No knowing,' he said. 'Someone blessedly ignorant, I'm relieved to say. Enoch did not try very hard to contradict my naïve assertion that the things were just common saddle pistols, so obviously he doesn't really know one way or the other.'

'Has he never heard about the loony earl?' Mr Kebble wore his most benign grin. It divided his exactly spherical face like a split across a ripe pumpkin.

The optician emitted one of his hums, which then turned into speech. 'Mm ... Mr Cartwright is scarcely one of our local luminaries in the matter of history. He's picked up some guff from somewhere about Purdy's the gunsmiths and the seventh earl of Flaxborough ...'

'James Scarbeck?' Mr Kebble interrupted.

'Scarbeck, yes. They were all crackers from him on, of course, but Jamie had the style that the rest of the barmy oafs lacked completely. And if Cartwright really knew the story about these pistols, he couldn't have resisted telling it.'

Mr Kebble sniffed the barrel of one. 'Never been fired, they say.'

'So the account goes.' Mr Hoole peered into the percussion cap recess. 'Ah – except for the one famous occasion.'

'But he's supposed never to have lost a duel.'

'Only because no one was ever crazy enough to accept a challenge from the fellow.' Mr Hoole clucked and hummed. 'Well, would you? Blunderbusses at ten paces? These things would mow half a cricket pitch on one charge.'

He regarded the weapons a little longer, then lovingly replaced them in their case. He tapped the engraved silver lozenge representing the Scarbeck family crest.

'The only bell-mouthed duelling pistols ever made, my dear Joss. Apart from their value as collectors' items, which is enormous, utterly vulgar, and a great deal more than poor Cartwright is going to ask for them, I think I shall cherish them mainly on account of the dear old Duke of Wellington.'

Mr Kebble beamed in pleasurable anticipation and rubbed a pencil between his palms so that it produced a rhythmic clicking noise against the two heavy gold rings that he wore. 'He was the one exception, was he?'

'He was. As one might expect. Our lunatic seventh earl got round to him in time and sent him one of his cartels ...'

'His what, old chap?'

'Cartels. Challenges. Carried personally by one's second, who was supposed to be able to help negotiate an honourable settle-ment. Except that Scarbeck always sent a most fearsome drunken illiterate with a great black beard, who insulted everyone in sight but couldn't be called out himself because he wasn't a gentleman. And invariably he took along the earl's bell-muzzles. The mere sight of that great case was enough to get an apology – even from some wretched fellow whom the loon had picked at random.'

At this point of the narrative, Sylvie approached bearing two cups of tea with slow and painful concentration. The offering pleased Mr Hoole so much that for a long time he lapsed into a mere intermittent hum while he stirred the tea and gazed vaguely through its steam.

The editor waited patiently, having pushed his own cup aside to cool. At last, 'And the Duke of Wellington?' he prompted.

Hoole stared at him for several seconds, then seemed suddenly to recall what he had been talking about. 'Ah, Old Nosey. That gentleman was not going to take any nonsense from some seedy, half-crazed aristocrat out of the sticks just because he carried a brace of cannon about with him. He accepted Scarbeck's chal-lenge and came over from Stamford, where he'd been staying the weekend. You know where they're supposed to have met, don't you?'

Mr Kebble shook his head and made a few more clicks with his pencil-rolling.

'In that low meadow-land on the other side of the river from the harbour. Quarrel Green, my dear fellow. The name tells all.' And Mr Hoole hummed in celebration of this piece of logic.

'But they didn't fight a duel, surely?'

'Not in the accepted sense, no. It was a notably effective en-counter, though. The Iron Duke made two vital stipulations that seemed, at first sight, to be very favourable to our James. He insisted that the seconds put a really generous charge of powder into each pistol. And also that the loony earl accept the privilege of first fire. Well, you see where that put Wellington.'

'In the shit,' suggested Mr Kebble.

Mr Hoole grinned. 'All the rules of honourable behaviour,' he said, 'plus the fact that not even an earl, crazy or not, could get away with blowing the head off the country's top national hero with a concessionary shot, obliged our James to delope.'

'De-what?'

'Delope. The duelling term for fire in the air.'

'And that's what he did?' Mr Kebble looked less than impressed.

'That's what he did, Joss. And the seventh earl of Flaxborough never sent out another challenge.'

'Too shamed?'

Mr Hoole's face grew even shinier. He was nodding with good humour. 'Lord, no. He made such a nice gesture of firing into the air with a dead straight arm that the recoil from that thundering great charge of powder smashed his wrist, fractured his elbow, and permanently dislocated his shoulder.'

There was a tinkle of laughter somewhere behind them. The editor swung his chair through a quarter-circle and peered over the tops of his glasses towards part of the area beyond the counter that was in the shadow of a tall display board. A young woman was standing there.

Mr Kebble stood at once, the plump and courteous uncle, friend of all 'totties', as he termed the whole of womankind from fourteen to fifty. He grinned a good morning and ran his fingers back through silky, daisy-white hair. 'Can I help you?'

'What a lovely story,' gurgled Miss Clemenceaux. 'Absolute blissikins. This the way in?' She had raised a flap in the counter and was side-stepping through the gap into the editorial enclosure.

Mr Kebble found a chair for her. She spiralled into it as if sitting down was a notable sensual accomplishment.

The optician regarded Birdie fixedly for some moments, his hands cradling his belly like a priest's.

'Mmm . . . are you a collector of Wellingtonia?' he asked.

'Boots, you mean?' Her bullet-hole eyes had expanded a little.

'Mmmm . . . anecdotes relating to Arthur Wellesley, first Duke of Wellington, the Iron one, so-called – Old Nosey. Mostly apocryphal, one suspects, but quite a character.'

'Especially with the artillery,' remarked Birdie, having picked up one of the pistols and grimaced prettily at its weight.

Mr Kebble tried to think of some homely observation to offset the discouraging effect he feared Hoole's academic chat might have upon the visiting tottie. He indicated the antique. 'Stick it up on end and you could put flowers in it, I suppose.'

'As the lady said to the gamekeeper,' Miss Clemenceaux observed, almost automatically. Mr Hoole said it was nice – and something of a novelty – to hear a well-turned literary allusion in Flaxborough. Was Miss Mmm . . . just passing through? On her way to the D. H. Lawrence country perhaps?

She smiled faintly and turned to the editor. 'Are you Mr Kebble?'

'I am.'

'Mr Josiah Kebble.' It was not a question. She framed the words commendingly, as a palaeontologist might read off the name of an unexpectedly well preserved fossil.

Mr Kebble chuckled. 'They tell me that when I was born it was the usual thing for parents to pick names by sticking pins in the Bible. I've a cousin who got Belial that way.'

Hoole looked delighted at the news. He turned to Birdie. 'Do you happen to be of a religious cast of mind, Miss Mmmm . . .?'

'I am a journalist.'

'That's nice,' exclaimed Mr Kebble, who did not think it nice at all but was anxious not to alienate someone who might prove to be an envoy – a spy, even – from the hateful head office in London. 'Would you like a cup of tea?'

She declined, but accepted one of the editor's battered cigarettes, which he offered her from a flat tobacco tin. 'My name's Birdie Clemenceaux. *Sunday Herald*. I'm a research assistant, actually. For Clive Grail.' She leaned back her head and sent slow curls of smoke from her nostrils, as if offering incense to that divinity.

Mr Kebble looked suitably impressed. The optician, though, smirked knowingly. 'Should I be in error, Miss, ah, Clemenceaux, in identifying the stock in trade of your periodical as a carefully balanced mixture of moral indignation and libidinous self-indulgence?'

If the little, round editor, who now stared at Birdie with an expression half amused and half alarmed, expected her to show resentment at this slur on her employers, he was disappointed. She simply confirmed, very soberly, that Mr Hoole's assessment was correct and that she could not have described the situation better herself.

27

'Unfortunately,' she went on, 'I am in hock, as it were, to these Machiavellian muck-spreaders and must serve their purposes or starve.'

Mr Kebble, who could not by the most extreme effort picture an emaciated Miss Clemenceaux, nodded sympathetically nevertheless.

'Which brings me,' she added, 'to the purpose of my calling on you, Mr Josiah Kebble.'

And suddenly the eyes were not holes any more but warm and lively lights in the midst of a smile. She's quite a nice little tottie, after all, reflected the editor. Had he not been a man with a highly developed sense of the ridiculous, he would have been much tempted to put his hand upon her knee. As it was, he just said, 'Yes, my dear?' in a tone of kindly encouragement, and hoped that Mr Hoole would soon desist from trying to hog the conversation.

'The fact is,' said Birdie, 'that my Mr Grail has been put into a very embarrassing position. Professionally, you understand. Not that I personally could lose much sleep over *that* – I mean, the man's an absolute tick – but we do happen to be a team, and we do sort of have to look after the bastard.'

'Of course, duckie.' Mr Kebble, who in his time had employed mutants of journalism ranging from a shop-lifter to a pyromaniac, knew how difficult loyalty could be sometimes.

'You see, we were coming through this village or whatever in the snob-wagon, minding our own business, when this lunatic copper tries to leap over the bonnet. Didn't touch him, actually, but Bob – he's our photographer – Bob was driving, and he's going to get done in court, and the publicity's going to be absolutely fiendish because of his association with the Clive Grail exposé-type column. I mean, Caesar's wife. All that. You do see.'

'Which Caesar?' hummed Mr Hoole, interested. 'There were lots of them, you know.'

The editor frowned. 'Are you sure you're not making too much of this?' he asked Birdie. 'I should have thought careless driving was the worst they could throw at your friend.'

'Actually . . .' The girl looked uncomfortable. 'Actually, the charge this copper's making isn't just that. It's something about driving at *him*. With intent, as they say. Of course, it's crazy.'

'What's the policeman's name? Did you notice?'

'Car . . . Cow . . .'

'Cowdrey?'

'That's it. Yes.'

'Barmy,' said Mr Kebble, very decidedly. 'His uncle was once the public hangman, they tell me. You mustn't worry about Baz, duckie. By the time your friend's in court again it'll be for failing to observe a traffic sign, or something.'

Mr Hoole, whose early expectations of academic responsiveness on the part of their visitor had been disappointed, was now wandering aimlessly around the office. The girl took the opportunity to lean closer to the editor and adopt a more serious and confidential tone.

'You're right, of course, but what we want to avoid is any mention of names at all – even in a local paper and in connection with a trivial traffic offence. There are people in Fleet Street who are keeping a bloody keen eye open for opportunities to make the *Sunday Herald* look foolish. They'd even use this.'

Mr Kebble's eyes widened at this intimation of professional skulduggery. After brief consideration, he said: 'You know better, of course, than to ask me to keep the case out of the paper.'

'Wouldn't dream of it,' averred Miss Clemenceaux, huskily. 'Surest way of getting it in.'

The editor nodded cheerfully. 'On the other hand, as a newspaperwoman you'll know that pressure of space does sometimes mean that some trivial item gets dished – always provided, mind you, that nobody's actually *asked* for it to be suppressed.'

'Ah, yes. That would be a horse of a different colour.' With which dashing equestrian metaphor, Birdie resumed her former attitude and expression just as Mr Hoole got back from his tour of the office.

Mr Kebble picked up his phone and called across to Carole to put him 'upstairs to Mr Prile', whereupon she pressed two or three switches sprouting from a box-like contraption beside her shopping-bag and then turned a little handle with every appearance of doubt and despondency.

There was a long, silent interval. Then Carole rose from her chair. 'I'll have to go up.' She disappeared through a door.

Mr Kebble, still nursing his phone, glanced at the ceiling.

'Supposed to have contracted sleeping sickness in Somalia,' he murmured in kindly explanation.

After another minute, the phone made noises suggestive of an imprisoned and much alarmed midget. Kebble spoke into it. 'It's all right, Kelvin; I just wanted to know if you'd picked up anything about a special court this afternoon . . . No? . . . No, don't bother, old chap, it was just a remand and I've got the details myself.'

He returned his attention to Birdie. 'There'll probably be another adjournment,' he said, 'but it will come into ordinary open court eventually. You realize that, of course, duckie.' His smile bespoke sad resignation.

Somewhat to Mr Kebble's surprise, the girl looked eminently satisfied. 'Grandikins!' she exclaimed. 'It's just this next fortnight that's a bit sensitive, actually. You've been a precious lamb, Mr Josiah Kebble.' And she swooped forward to nuzzle a cheek against the centre of Mr Kebble's pink, shiny forehead.

When she had pranced away, having blown a valedictory kiss to Mr Hoole, Mr Kebble remarked chucklesomely what a nice little tottie she was.

The optician regarded him with wry amusement for a few seconds, then turned his attention to one of the pistols. 'Mmm . . . yes . . .' He squinted into the bell of its barrel. 'You really must try, some time, Joss, to view people through the eye of the entomologist.'

'Oh, aye?' Mr Kebble's expression of extreme geniality was unchanged. 'And what should I have seen in that particular little ladybird?'

Mr Hoole pouted, sniffed, said nothing.

Chapter Four

A CONVERSATION WAS BEING HELD AT THE SAME TIME, and about the same person and her friends, in the office of Inspector Purbright at Fen Street police headquarters.

Sergeant Love sounded quite excited. 'You know who he is,

don't you? Not the bloke Baz arrested – his pal, the big, smarmy-looking one.'

'Apart from his bearing the rather unlikely name of Grail, I'm afraid I don't, Sid. Why, is he a pop singer or something?'

The inspector's other-worldliness earned a grimace of exasperation from the sergeant. 'No, it's Grail of the *Sunday Herald*. He's a right stirrer, that one.' A sudden gleam in Love's youthful eye made him look more than ever like a schoolboy autograph-hunter. 'Didn't you see that piece last Sunday?'

Purbright confessed that he had not. Bill Malley, though, made good his deprivation at once. 'God, aye – the bit about the nude dollies at the tax inspectors' conference at Swansea.'

'They reckon that lad can topple governments,' added Love, with sober conviction.

'Look out, Flaxborough chamber of trade,' murmured Purbright.

A hopeful grin lifted a couple of the coroner's officer's chins. 'This little brush with Baz Cowdrey isn't going to make Mr Grail very friendly. Perhaps he'll put something in the paper about the sauna at the Klub Kissinger.'

'Or the probation officer's dirty postcard trade,' added Love, warming to the spirit of the thing.

'Ah, that's only among his own clients,' pointed out the inspector. 'Be fair, Sid.'

'What I don't understand,' said Malley, 'is what this bunch was doing in the town in the first place. They're still here, you know. Or just outside. Herbert Stamper's rented them that place of his on the Chalmsbury Road.'

Purbright allowed a short break in his maintenance of an air of being unimpressed. 'God, *there's* a gentleman who'd be a natural for the *Sunday Herald*.'

'A bit of a lad, old Stamper,' commented Sergeant Love.

'They say one of his housekeepers is looking after that London party,' Malley informed them.

'*One* of his housekeepers? How many does Mr Stamper run to?'

It was Love's turn to grin. 'On the Fen, they reckon he uses a sort of rotation principle. Like fields. The one he's lent out has probably been lying fallow.'

The inspector looked at him reprovingly. 'You've been spending too much time with your fiancée's disgusting agricultural relatives, Sid. Anyway,' he glanced at the clock, 'I think we might call it a day.'

Sergeant Malley, who never disengaged from a conversation with anything like dispatch, was rubbing his right ear thoughtfully. 'I'd still like to know what this Grail character and his friends are hoping to dig up in Flax. They don't move a couple of hundred miles out of London just for a change of air.'

Purbright gave him a tight smile, a pat on the shoulder, and was gone. Love hesitated a moment, then shrugged and followed the inspector.

Farmer Herbert Stamper sat at the wheel of his big Mercedes motor car and gazed aside with great satisfaction at the straggles of yellowing sugar beet on the land of a rival who had neglected to apply a preventative spray at the appropriate time. He was driving slowly – at no more than twenty miles an hour – in the middle of the highway that led eventually to Chalmsbury and the coast. Following traffic was obliged to form a procession whose leisurely pace was woefully inconsistent with the patience of the participants. The drivers of approaching cars had no choice but to veer off into the sanctuary of the grass verge, where they wound down windows, shook fists, and shouted imprecations of a violent and obscene kind. Hearing these as a mere murmur through the heavy tinted glass of his mobile pavilion, Farmer Stamper smiled. He liked people to swear at him. It proved that he was still doing well in life.

A couple of miles out of town, Farmer Stamper made a right-angle turn into a lane very suddenly and without giving a signal, and was agreeably cursed by his retinue.

The lane led between two colonnades of elms to a big square house of bright red brick. This house had been recently built at Stamper's behest but with care that his name should appear on none of the documents connected with its construction and purchase. Its intended function, as such circumspect measures might suggest, was that of doxy-box, or, in other words, accommodation for whichever housekeeper of the moment might be receiving Mr Stamper's special favours. Unfortunately, his chronically ailing but vigilant wife had got wind of the enterprise and now made spot checks from time to time to ensure that whoever was enjoying the facilities of Mr Stamper's investment, it was not its proprietor. She had set the seal of her supervision upon the building by insisting upon its being named, after her, 'MIRIAM LODGE'.

He parked the Mercedes at a clumsy angle across the front of Grail's Rolls and emerged heavily, as from the cab of a tractor. The door he swung shut behind him with his boot as he stared up at the house. A survey of the windows, first of the bedrooms then those on the ground floor, took him only a few seconds. He trudged across the gravel to the front door and gave it a hearty thump with its lion's head knocker.

The door was opened by a woman of about the same height as Stamper. Under black, untidy hair, was a lean, well-weathered face; the mouth wide, not ungenerous, but tightened by a sort of grim amusement that could have betokened a long and mainly successful struggle for independence. The chin and cheekbones were sharply angular, the nose narrow, straight and red-ridged by exposure to the winter winds of the fen country. Her eyes were half closed for the same reason; they were steady, though, and almost impertinently speculative.

The name of this lady was Lily Patmore.

She addressed the owner of the house. 'Now, then, y'old bugger.'

Farmer Stamper was not a man to give vocal expression to his emotions, but as he pushed past Mrs Patmore into the hallway he cupped one of his great hands about her bottom and honked it good-naturedly.

'I see Mawksley's beet's doing bloody badly. If there's one acre with the yellows, there must be bloody forty.'

The housekeeper observed that sugar beet wouldn't be the only thing to suffer if he didn't give up making free with her arse, whereupon Mr Stamper offered to wemble her: a proposition that moved Mrs Patmore to remark that his persistence in pawming her when there was company in the house was simply begging for a kick in the lesk.

At which point in their amatory exchange, a door opened so suddenly behind them that both jumped as guiltily as poachers.

Turning, they saw the newspaperman, Ken Lanching. He was holding a twelve-bore shotgun.

Stamper stumped towards him, waving his hand down. 'Never you hold a bloody gun like that, son. You'll have some bugger's head off.'

Lanching lowered the barrels until they nearly touched the floor. He kept hold of the stock with obvious reluctance. 'It was over the fireplace,' he said. 'I don't suppose it's loaded.'

'Of course it's bloody loaded,' Stamper retorted. 'What good's a bloody gun wi'out?' He took the weapon, broke it to check that both cartridges were in place, and strode into the dining-room. Effortlessly with one hand he lifted the gun back on its hooks.

'Where's your mates?'

Lanching looked slightly bewildered by the question. 'Oh, around,' he said.

'Everything all right? Lil's seeing to you, is she?' Mr Stamper seemed not to require answers. He winked. 'Mind you don't try and see to *her*, though.' A nod towards the housekeeper. 'Eh, Lil?'

Mrs Patmore glanced aloft with mock patience and left the room.

'Where's your Mr Grail?' inquired Stamper, suddenly business-like. Lanching said he had gone out for a walk but would soon be back.

The farmer gave an appraising stare around the room while he asked casually: 'You're managing all right, then, are you? Finding what you wanted to know?'

'Well, more or less . . .'

'I must say,' said Stamper, approvingly feeling the texture of the wallpaper with fingers as big as dinner rolls, 'that I can't think of anything in bloody Flax as'd interest a newspaper in London.'

Lanching shrugged uncertainly. 'Oh, I wouldn't say that. It depends.'

The farmer gave him a long stare. 'You know,' he said at last, 'I reckon you're the recklin of this bloody litter.'

'The what?'

'Recklin. The weakest. The one as won't make bacon.' He pronounced it '*baya*con' with a diphthong that sounded as if it were being dragged through heavy loam.

'I can't say I have any ambitions in that line.' Stamper grunted.

'That lass of yourn's not as green as she's cabbage-looking, though. I'll bet she keeps you lot snaped.'

'Keeps us . . . ?'

'*Snaya*ped.' (Again the laboured diphthong.) 'Under control. Ready to jump when she tells you.'

Lanching clearly found translation difficulties too substantial to permit of argument.

The farmer plunged into even more outrageous speculation. 'Whose tottie is she, anyway?' he demanded. 'I'd not like to cause trouble by getting it wrong. Which one's serving her – the boss?'

'Boss?' echoed Lanching, praying for rescue from this importunate hayseed.

'Gaffer,' explained Stamper. 'Top man. Grail. The one who writes the pieces in the paper. She's *his* little bed-tommy, is she?'

'I know nothing of Miss Clemenceaux's relationships, and I can't say I'm wildly interested.'

Stamper regarded him as if he were beginning to show signs of incipient stem wilt. 'Not wildly interested. Ah.' He turned his attention to a sideboard on which several bottles of spirits were set out. 'Cost three hundred and eighty five quid, did that. Four years back.' One of the great fingers explored the surface. 'You want to put some bloody newspaper on it before something gets spilt and snerps the polish.'

Lanching started towards the door. 'If there's anything else you want, Mr Stamper . . .'

The farmer did not look round. He said to the bottle of gin he had picked up: 'What's your friend Grail want with Alf Blossom, then?'

'Blossom?'

'South Circuit Garage. Asked me where it was. Among other things. Why should he want to know that?'

'No idea.'

'Thought it was the tottie who turned your top soil.'

'Miss Clemenceaux is the research assistant, if that's what you mean.'

'Aye, well, now *I've* put a spade in, mister. P'raps I'll get *my* name in the paper.' Stamper put down the gin bottle and picked up one of whisky. As he squinted through it against the light from the window, he threw out another of his blunt, apparently aimless questions. 'What do you reckon to the boss asking me if I know who's the secretary of the Flaxborough bloody Camera Club?'

'Why shouldn't he ask you, if that was what he wanted to know?'

'Well your mate's the snapshot man, isn't he? Not Grail. Struck me he's got a harse-forrard way of doing things.'

Someone was crossing the hall. Stamper went to the door and looked out. He stepped back a moment later to admit Clive Grail, who was closely followed by Mrs Patmore.

'There's some dinner ready if you'd like to come through,' she said, carefully angling the invitation to by-pass Stamper. The farmer tap-tippied one of her breasts with the backs of his fingers in the manner of a vet, and started to leave.

From the other side of the doorway he called back: 'That club secretary. Draper Pearce. Harry.' Footsteps receded heavily, as if over furrows.

'You mustn't mind him,' Mrs Patmore said to Grail. 'His dad's worse. And *he's* pushing ninety. The warden's wife will never go on her own into that old folk's bungalow of his.'

Grail, who did not appear much heartened by this information, gave Lanching a perplexed look. 'What was he talking about? Who is Pearce?'

'You asked him the name of the secretary of some local photography club, didn't you? They make films, or try to.'

Grail's hand rose immediately to riffle through his silky, silvery-grey hair. 'God, yes! I'd forgotten.' He turned to the housekeeper. 'Do you know this gentleman Harry Pearce, Mrs Patmore?'

'Not ever so well. He used to keep a shop but it's been taken over by Brown and Derehams. His wife's one of the Harrison girls, but you'd not think it to look at her now. Of course, it was Harry who got mixed up with some rather nasty goings on in that Folklore Society or whatever they called themselves. I always thought he was a bit of an old woman, myself. Still, I don't suppose you . . .'

'No, not really,' Grail interjected mildly.

Unoffended, Mrs Patmore completed Mr Pearce's biography, as she understood it, and added as bonus the news that he once had discovered a body.

Grail was by then sorting some pages of typescript that he had taken from a slim leather case. He favoured the housekeeper with a bright, if brief glance and an encouraging 'Oh, yes?'

'Well, not to say body, exactly,' she amended. 'She did die soon afterwards, though. That was photography. Poor Edie. Well, I expect you remember it. It was all in the papers.'

'So it was,' murmured Grail automatically. This time he did not look up.

Lanching appeared much puzzled by the ascribing of the mysterious Edie's death to 'photography'. Some time later, he again brought up the subject. Birdie Clemenceaux and Becket had returned and all four had eaten Mrs Patmore's substantial offering of a game casserole and an apple and elderberry pudding, of which even the normally abstemious Grail had accepted a second helping. Lanching, happily somnolent, eyed his coffee. 'A bit odd, the old girl's story about that woman,' he said.

'What woman?' Birdie asked. She looked at the others. 'What old girl, for that matter?'

'Oh, of course. You weren't here. Mrs Whatsername – the housekeeper – she was burbling on about photography and a woman getting poisoned.'

'Edith Bush, you mean.' Birdie gave a slight shrug. 'So?'

Grail said: 'It was in the London evenings. Didn't you notice it, Ken?' His tone was casual, but the interjection had come very promptly. Lanching looked at him uncertainly.

'Yes, but the story we're on up here . . .' He turned to Birdie. 'You knew her name. When I mentioned poisoning just now, you came straight out with it. Edith Bush. As if it was familiar.'

'Well, of course it was. Heavens, the story ran for several days.' Birdie scooped a fourth spoonful of sugar into her coffee. The look she gave Lanching was lazy, amused.

'Names – some stick, some don't. It doesn't signify,' said Grail, smoothly.

Lanching glanced down the room at Becket, as if in appeal, but Becket appeared to be taking no interest in anything beyond his own knees, which he had hitched up against the edge of the table and was regarding fixedly with an expression of absent-minded gloom.

'Very well, then,' Lanching said at last. 'Don't bloody tell me if you don't want to.'

Grail sighed. 'It's not a question of not telling you anything, Ken. The stuff I'm doing up here . . .'

'The stuff *we're* doing.' Lanching's somnolence had evaporated.

'All right. We. Sure. The stuff *we* are doing is what I told you – a straight exposé feature . . .'

'The wicked burgers of Little England,' Birdie explained. 'Quailing before Grail's flail.'

From Grail, a nod of gracious indulgence. 'Miss Tit-brain expresses the matter precisely,' he said to Lanching. 'My column – oh, with your help, dear colleagues, with your most valuable help – my column, I say, is devoted exclusively to the one and only object that justifies the existence of the cant-ridden, meretricious old harlot that we call the Press. That object being? Right, dearly beloved. Muck-raking.'

All of which was said in a gentle, beautifully modulated voice and accompanied by the delicate gesturing of long, alabastine fingers.

'Mr Stamper,' said Lanching, 'asked me if you two were lovers.'

'Oh, blissikins!' trilled Miss Clemenceaux.

Bob Becket slowly slid his regard from his knees to Grail's face.

Grail looked more beatific than usual. 'Salt of the earth, is Mr Stamper. Have you noticed how he blows steam from his nostrils?' He paused, then said, half to himself: 'I wonder if the art of the cinema is among his passions.'

In another room, a telephone began ringing. Grail turned his chair from the table, as if in expectation. And it was to him that Mrs Patmore soon afterwards imparted the message that he was required by a gentleman speaking from London.

Immediately Grail had left the room, Lanching leaned forward across the table and spoke hurriedly to Becket. 'Hey, Bob, you've kept bloody quiet up to now. Just what exactly are we supposed to be getting into? One minute I'm being told to chat up some old birds in an amateur photographic society, and the next I get briefed on how to point a shotgun if anyone walks in without knocking.'

'Briefed? Who briefed you?'

Lanching jerked his head towards Grail's empty chair. 'The holy father.'

'He hasn't got a shotgun,' said Birdie.

'Well, what do you think that is, hanging over the fireplace? A vacuum cleaner?'

'That's an antique,' said Becket. 'Like carriage lamps and that sort of crap.'

'It's a double-barrelled twelve-bore,' said Lanching firmly. 'And it's got two shells ready to go off.'

Birdie regarded the weapon with a little wrinkle of distaste.

'It's Stamper who keeps it loaded,' explained Lanching.

This information appeared to come as no surprise to Becket. 'I tell you,' he said bitterly, 'they have a homicidal streak round here. Police. Farmers. All of them. You talk about muggings in London. But at least London's got bloody lights. You go outside this house and you might as well be in the Underground during a power cut.'

Mrs Patmore, entering to clear the dishes, expressed the hope that they had had enough belly-timber. She added – seemingly with reference to Birdie's having left her potatoes untasted – that she'd never grow much of a kedge if she didn't eat her orts – an assurance which Birdie decided to accept smilingly as a compliment. Whereupon Mrs Patmore roguishly observed to the company at large that young Mistress Grail wouldn't be able to blame tates when the time came for her to be in calf, would she?

'Oh, Christ!' said Miss Clemenceaux, when the housekeeper had borne away her great piled tray. 'She thinks I'm Mrs Pius XIII.'

'That impression,' Lanching said, 'seems remarkably general in these parts. Perhaps there's an amorous side to Clive's nature that shows up only in the clear air of the country. Our vision is clouded by cynicism and gin.'

Becket, to whom these remarks seemed to have been particularly addressed and who looked very cross, was just opening his mouth to speak when Grail appeared in the doorway. He had just quiffed a hank of his soft hair attractively over one side of his brow with the little nursery brush he kept always in an inner side pocket for that purpose. He looked even more likely than usual to be on the point of calling for volunteers in his audience to come out for Jesus. In the event, however, he said merely: 'That was Richardson. The prelim is set and it's already gone into the early editions.' He pulled one of the chairs away from the table and sat, his long, thin legs crossed and his head on one side in an attitude of dreamy abstraction while he delicately plied a toothpick.

Birdie spoke to him. 'Have they used all the stuff you sent? *As you sent it?*'

'Naturally. My copy stands as it goes. Always.' The toothpick moved to a further site.

'In that case . . .' Becket suddenly set his chair with a crash upon its full complement of legs and sat upright himself for the first time since finishing his meal. 'In that case, let's hope that we collect some better evidence than we've managed to root out so far. These bloody people are lynchers. I'm bloody sure of it.'

Grail turned up his calm, martyr's smile. 'Well, now; isn't that a nice incentive for you all.' He paused, as if to enjoy their discomfiture, then said: 'Don't despair. I bring you good news. Richardson says that the Kuwait film has now reached the office. They are getting a print sent up here as soon as they can. Won't that be a jolly job for us?' It was Birdie now who was receiving the full benefit of the smile.

'Christ!' Becket lit a cigarette with such furious haste that it immediately went out again. He drew on it twice, then threw it in his coffee. 'I'd have thought we'd got a bit past that stage of getting a thrill.'

The outburst left Grail looking genuinely perplexed. He soon recovered, however.

'My dear Bob, I'm sorry. No one who knows you would suggest for a moment that you are in need of puerile stimulus of that order. My promise is not of vicarious sex, but of that very evidence the lack of which you were deploring just now.

'I have – no, *we* have – set up in tomorrow's edition the skeleton from the, ah – what is it again? – ah yes, Flaxborough – the skeleton from the Flaxborough cupboard; but next week, if, as I am confident you will, you do your work well, those bones will be clothed in flesh – in identifiable flesh. And then let's see who talks of lynching, eh?'

Chapter Five

THE MAYOR OF FLAXBOROUGH ENJOYED A NUMBER OF privileges appropriate to his office, including a pair of ornamental lamp standards outside his red brick semi-villa in Birtley Avenue, but he received his Sunday newspapers with no more ceremony than other citizens; like them, he came downstairs in his pyjamas and collected his weekend reading in person from where it had been tossed disrespectfully and sometimes inaccurately in the vicinity of his front door.

Thus attired, and displaying that humpy, trundley disposition peculiar to Sunday awakenings, Alderman Charles Hockley looked more like a hippopotamus than ever as he stood at his porch and blinked the tiny eyes that seemed perpetually in peril of disappearing for good.

He bent and assembled the papers in some sort of order before scooping the pile under one arm. Only as he turned and re-entered the house did something he had seen register sharply on his consciousness. He dumped the load of newsprint on the hall table, rapidly sorted through it, and pulled one paper free.

It was the *Sunday Herald*. And heading the last two columns of the front page was a picture of an everyday street scene in an ordinary English town. Or so it would have appeared to an ordinary reader. But Alderman Hockley stood in special relationship to the town depicted. He was Mayor of it.

And yet . . . Could this be Flaxborough, this row of small shops on one side of a market place, these stalls, this familiar-seeming hotel? Mr Hockley read the astonishing legend, or manifesto, or whatever it was, beneath the photograph; stared at the incredible headlines; and once again scrutinized the picture.

Yes, it was Flax, all right. Not a doubt of it. There was Semple's music shop. And the Farmers' Union offices. And a dead clear likeness of old Peters crossing the road by the whelk and winkle stall.

But no mention of the name of the place.

'Margaret!' The cry that issued in a raucous Scots accent from the twenty-one stone frame of Alderman Hockley sounded like a summons to quit a burning building before the roof fell in, but in fact he had raised it without even the effort of taking his eyes from the paper.

From upstairs came a muffled and somewhat indifferent acknowledgment. The mayoress was used to her husband's off-stage alarms.

'The ratepayers'll be up in arms when they read this!' declared the mayor at the same pitch. He moved on into the kitchen, still scanning Mr Grail's tantalizing promises of 'a full and frank exposure of this quiet little town's Club of Shame', and put the kettle on.

Mr Hockley, whose continued enjoyment of the defunct title of alderman was due, in his special case, to its having become a sort of good-humoured tribute to his bulk and pomposity, had emigrated to Flaxborough from his native Glasgow some forty years previously. He now was head of a timber firm that made his family so much money so easily that he was able to devote his full time and not inconsiderable energy to public benefaction.

This took several forms. He sat, for instance, on a whole clutch of committees that had been laid by the Town Council, the Conservative and Unionist Association, the Dogs at Sea Society and sundry other zealots in the canine interest. He was one of the Grammar School governors and the vice-chairman of the League of Friends of Flaxborough Hospital. He also was a leading member of one of those bands of emigré Scotsmen who gather once a year in every English town to mourn, in whisky, sheepgut and oatmeal, their sufferance of prosperity in exile.

Charlie Hockley, moreover, was an indefatigable champion of worthy causes in an individual capacity. He was a generous subscriber to charity and needed to be subjected to only the sketchiest of pleading to be convinced of some fraud, injustice or imposition, and thereupon to 'speak out', as he termed it, without further investigation. This quixotic impulsiveness had led, more than once, to embarrassment, such as that which resulted from his 'speaking out' against the severity of a prison sentence recently imposed by the Flaxborough Bench, quite forgetting that he himself had presided on that occasion in his mayoral capacity as chief magistrate.

Mr Hockley's imaginary allies in his forays were those very

ratepayers whom he had invoked a few moments previously; worthy, if choleric citizens who spent their lives in a constant state of readiness to take up arms.

Such supposition was, of course, utterly delusory. There had been no instance of civil strife in Flaxborough since the 1893 election, when an attempt by the authorities to close the pubs and thus interfere with the traditional bribery of the voters with strong drink resulted in every policeman in sight being rounded up and locked for the rest of the day and night in one of the town's bonded warehouses.

The truth was that Alderman Hockley was a general without an army, but people had grown so used to the spectacle of his indignant bravura on the redoubt of municipal politics that their question: 'What's the old bugger on about now?' was prompted by quite amiable regard and even a modicum of genuine interest.

'Whatever,' asked the mayoress on her arrival, dressing-gowned and yawning, at the kitchen door, 'are you on about now, Charlie?'

He jabbed a fat forefinger at the *Herald*'s front page. 'Just you wait,' he said. 'The whole town –'

'– will be up in arms. Come on, mind out of the way and perhaps we can get a cup of tea.'

Fortunately for Mr Hockley, there were available in Flaxborough more tolerant listeners than his wife. After breakfast, he bore down upon the telephone like a fat old roué about to embrace a complaisant mistress.

Upon anyone of less volatile temperament than His Worship and of keener analytical sense, the *Herald* article might not have made its intended impression. It possessed all the elements of evangelical journalism: its tendentiousness, its coyness in the matter of actual places, dates and names, its reliance upon the propulsive power of moral indignation to carry the account safely over swamps of imprecision and chasms of missing fact. It was distinctly tainted, furthermore, with that curious odour – as of some kind of moral Athlete's Foot – which any old Fleet Street man will recognize as a product of ethical acrobatics.

The mayor's first victim was Mr Dampier-Small, deputy town clerk. The holder of the substantive office was, as always when telephoned by Alderman Hockley, 'most unfortunately out of town – can I get him to ring you?' His deputy, as was only proper, did not run to a well trained, mendacious wife.

'Yes, sir. As a matter of fact, I do happen to have read it. A most offensive piece, I thought.'

'Offensive? I'm glad you think it's offensive, laddie. I'll tell you this, and no messing. The town is going to be up in arms about it.' And Mr Hockley's scarlet dewlap flapped up and down like a turkey's wattles.

'It does seem a somewhat unfortunate outburst,' said Mr Dampier-Small. 'Although, of course, the town is not identified – not in so many words. Legal response might be tricky, Mr Mayor. Quite tricky.'

'But there's a picture of the place. Right here in the paper. I know my own town when I see it. You're not going to tell me I don't know my own town?'

Oh, God, thought Mr Dampier-Small, why does this lunatic have to be sicked on to me every time? 'Ha ha,' he said, trying to sound fruitily humorous, 'I would need to get up early in the morning to tell you that!'

'What's getting up early to do with it?' inquired Mr Hockley, genuinely mystified.

There was an uncomfortable pause.

'Never mind that,' resumed the mayor, 'what I want to know is what we're going to do about this . . . this pack of lies in the paper.'

'With respect, Mr Mayor, there would not seem to be sufficient in the way of definite, ah, assertion – yes, definite assertion – in the article to constitute anything actionable.' Another pause, shorter. 'If I make myself clear.'

Mr Hockley shuddered with righteous exasperation and pushed aside the mayoress, who was trying to give him a cup of tea. 'Now listen, Mister Deputy Town Clerk, and I quote. Are you listening? Right. And I quote. "World Copyright Reserved . . ." – you know what that means? It means this stuff is going all over the globe, that's what that means. "World Copyright . . ." Wait a minute . . . Aye, listen to this – and I quote. "When I arrived in this pleasant, sleepy little market town, writes Clive Grail, the *Sunday Herald*'s special reporter on the state of the nation's moral health" – and he's the fellow you have to get after, Mr DTC, not a doubt of that – "I thought to myself that here was likely to be found a community still conforming in pattern with the old yeoman stock that won England's acres" – no, now wait a minute, that's not the part I wanted to read out . . . Aye, here we are – and I quote . . .'

Twenty minutes of this mainly one-sided conversation left the deputy town clerk in a good deal more exhausted state than that in which he had gone to bed the night before. He had failed utterly either to understand what Mr Hockley supposed could be done about the scurrilous assertions of the man Grail, or – and this was more worrying – to fathom why he, a responsible and respected officer of municipal government, could allow himself to be hectored at Sunday breakfast time by an obese Scottish floor-board merchant scarcely capable of signing his own name.

As soon as he could escape from the mayor's imprecations, which grew less articulate as they gained in ire, Mr Dampier-Small drank three cups of strong coffee and composed himself to re-read the *Herald*'s article more attentively. He was by now in a mood to hope that allegations which had so grievously offended Mr Hockley were true – indeed, that they might prove the mere tip of a monstrous iceberg of moral delinquency that would crush once and for all the vulgar self-righteousness of the mayor and burgesses of Flaxborough.

Meanwhile, the mayor's rallying cry was speeding over the wire to Queen's Road, where the chief constable had most grudgingly interrupted a curry-combing session with his pack of Yorkshire terriers in order to receive the intelligence that the town was up in arms.

'It seems to me,' Alderman Hockley was declaring to him, 'that the main target for this fellow's abuse – and it's very offensive abuse, let me tell you, Mr Chubb, very offensive – his main target, I said, is the Flaxborough Photographic Society.'

'Really?' responded Mr Chubb, with an expression suggestive of his having been told that Mrs Chubb had just been arrested for soliciting. He in fact was not interested in anything that the mayor had said or was likely to say that morning, but knew from past experience that to admit indifference simply fed the furnace of Mr Hockley's zeal.

'You,' stated Mr Hockley – and Mr Chubb could almost feel the man's finger poking him in the chest – 'you are a member of the Photographic Society, Mr Chief Constable. The vicar is a member. I don't think I tell a lie when I say he's on the committee. As I am. Yours truly. And it's nothing short of disgraceful and disgusting that a Sunday newspaper is allowed to print this sort of thing.' A slight pause. 'You've read this, of course?'

Mr Chubb had not. He said: 'One of my officers is detailed to go through the items in the Press. He doubtless will give me a report a little later. I believe, however . . .' He paused to let pass, like the tiniest of sighs, a scruple, then: 'I believe that Inspector Purbright takes this particular newspaper. Should you feel the matter to be of urgency, Mr, ah . . .'

'I'll get on to him right away, Mr Chief Constable. It doesn't do to let grass grow under our feet when this sort of thing happens. Listen, you may not believe this, but four people have stopped me in the street already this morning and asked what the police are doing about it.'

Two minutes later, Mr Chubb was squatting in carefree communion with his dogs while half a mile away a telephone rang at 15 Tetford Drive, the home, but not the refuge, of Detective Inspector Purbright.

'This is the mayor speaking, Mr Inspector. About this article in the *Herald*. You might find this hard to believe, but ten people – ten ratepayers – have called at my house already this morning and asked what's being done about it.'

Purbright slipped three fingers over the mouthpiece and half whispered, half mimed to his wife: 'It's Rob Roy. The town's up in arms again.' Ann Purbright resignedly went back to the kitchen and removed a pan of half-cooked rashers and kidneys from beneath the grill.

One man only in the entire town there was who could be said to be eagerly expectant of a call from Alderman Hockley. That was Josiah Kebble. And although it was almost noon, Mr Kebble's brandy and water hour, before the spreading telephonic wave of mayoral indignation reached the editor's house, he received the confidence that more than thirty ratepayers (many of them professional men) had called in person upon Mr Hockley to urge action, with an air of spontaneous surprise and sympathy that was altogether gratifying.

46

The truth was that Mr Kebble, like many another newspaper editor, fed his readers, whenever possible, upon such tasty or exciting sentiments as he could induce some public figure or other to express. He was, in a sense, a professional opener of other men's mouths, yet would have modestly disclaimed any skill in the matter, holding that so many notable members of the community were permanently agape with their own opinions that a reporter had only to listen, select and record.

'This is a terrible slur on the town's good name,' declared Mr Kebble, eyeing his drink against the light from the window. He appeared very happy despite the lamentable tidings.

'Aye, you're right there, Jossie. And I don't intend to let it rest; you can be sure of that.'

'Of course, as mayor . . .' Mr Kebble took a sip of his brandy and water, giving silence a chance to prime Hockley's expectancy.

'Aye?'

'I'd have thought that, as mayor, you are in a very special position to put these London scandal-mongers in their place.'

'You think so?'

'The readers will certainly think so,' declared the editor of the *Citizen*, *ex cathedra*.

Mr Hockley stroked his dewlap reflectively. No doubt about it: Kebble was a good man, a first-rater. 'A strong statement – an official statement. From the mayor.' The effort of composition deeply furrowed Hockley's brow. 'You know – refuting the, the what, the lies – no, the distortions, the outrageous . . .'

Mr Kebble took aim with the notion he had been fashioning ever since his eye had fallen delightedly upon Grail's story in the *Herald*.

'May I,' he interrupted, 'put forward something rather unconventional, Mr Mayor? Something, if I may say so, that is just your style?'

Mr Hockley, had he possessed any latitude in the matter of expansion, might be said at that moment to have swelled.

'That's exactly what I like, Jossie,' he declared. 'The unexpected. The one right in the belly. Heh?' The high Caledonian cackle of glee came oddly from his huge, swarthy face. Hearing it, even without the benefit of seeing the face, Mr Kebble winced and reinforced himself with another swig of brandy and water.

47

'I take it that the town isn't wrong in looking on you as a sportsman,' he went on.

'No-o-o – oh, no, no. Not wrong at all. Not at all, Jossie. Make no mistake about that.'

Mr Kebble grunted approbation. 'Mind you,' he added, with the air of a bookie offering ridiculously long odds on a certain winner, 'this could land you with the hell of a lot of publicity – national publicity. You might not care for that, even if the town did benefit as a result.'

The mayor slipped immediately into his hand-on-heart manner. 'All I want, Mr Editor – and you can take it from me that I'm not one for the bull and the flannel – you know that, don't you? – aye, you know that fine. All I want, I say, is for this wicked pack of nonsense in the paper to be taken back. Denied. Refuted. An apology's what I want. And it's what I'm going to get, make no mistake about that. I dare this fellow – what's his name again? . . .'

'Grail.'

'Aye, Grail – I dare him to show his face here while I'm mayor of this town. He needn't think I'm too old to do a bit of horse-whipping.'

'What I had in mind,' said Mr Kebble, thoughtfully, 'did happen to be something in the nature of a direct personal challenge. The public like that sort of thing. It gets through to them much better than official statements.'

'Fine, old friend! Fine! I'm game. I'll challenge him, all right, make no mistake about that. Look, what do you say to coming round here so that we can work something up. Heh? You're better at words than I am. And they'll need to be good for this little job! Heh?'

It was not far from the editor's house to the mayoral residence. He went by bicycle. Mr Kebble rode a cycle with as much panache as a squire might ride his hunter. Instead of field gear, though, he wore his unvarying costume of leather-elbowed tweed jacket, trousers like twin bags of oatmeal and the editorial waistcoat whose host of pockets accommodated useful equipment that ranged from a portable balance for weighing fish to a goldsmith's touchstone. His hat, a carefully preserved relic of journalism in the 20's, was a stiff, creamy-grey felt, high-crowned and broad of brim, which perched far back on his head to give full display to

48

the round, pink, mischievously amiable face.

The mayor, still in his dressing gown, was waiting hospitably at his front door. He helped Mr Kebble dismount and propped his bicycle against one of the ceremonial lamp standards.

They went together to the somewhat overblown room with feathery furnishings in pale blue and gold that Mrs Hockley still called the lounge but which her husband, more readily adaptable to protocol, designated the Mayor's Parlour.

Mr Kebble made himself comfortable at once, sinking into a divan like a quicksand trimmed with blue grass. Alderman Hockley, still too agitated to sit, spent some time fussing to and from a drinks cabinet with two empty glasses in his hands. His main difficulty, it seemed, lay in persuading himself that Kebble really had asked for brandy in preference to Scotch whisky. 'Are you poorly, Jossie?' he kept asking.

The point at last was settled.

'Cheers,' said Mr Kebble. The ride had given him a thirst.

The mayor raised his glass with a flourish. 'Here's to our little town, aye, and may its good name soon be restored.'

The editor concealed behind a patient, round-faced grin his dislike, developed over a long career of reporting public dinners, of what he called 'wind-and-piss sentiments'.

Then, after having given Mr Hockley a minute or two to recover from the emotional stimulus of his own toast, he set about his task.

'Tell me, Mr Mayor,' said Mr Kebble, with the gravest expression of interest, 'tell me – have you ever thought of fighting a duel?'

Chapter Six

THE FOLLOWING MORNING, THERE ARRIVED AT THE rented retreat of Clive Grail and his colleagues a *Sunday Herald* staff car. The driver, a Londoner in whose estimation anywhere as distant from the capital as Flaxborough was dangerously near the unfenced brink of the world, got out and made a rapid, nervous survey of the house and its setting before going up to the front door.

He told Mrs Patmore that he was from the office and had brought some gear and that Mr Grail or somebody had better lend a hand and show him where it had to be put.

'What gear?' asked Mrs Patmore, whose private view was strengthening daily that her obligation to Mr Stamper should not include ministering to the unpredictable and sometimes quite unreasonable demands of what she called 'that newspaper lot'.

Just a film and projector and stuff, the driver said, but it was heavy and he wasn't going to rupture himself on top of a morning of being misdirected by a bunch of idiots who couldn't speak English.

At which point, Grail appeared at the door and looked pleasantly surprised. 'Hello, Tone!' he said.

'Heh, wossorl this abaht a dool, then?' inquired the driver, with reciprocally approving recognition.

'Dool?'

'Yeah, dool. Wiv some mayor geyser. Pistols at dorn'norl that. Sin the bladdy mile. Sun'norl.'

Tone illustrated the truth of this statement by producing from various pockets closely folded copies of the *Daily Mail* and the *Sun*. '*And* the bladdy garjun,' he added, with a sneer, but in this case without the evidence.

'Yes, I did see something in the *Guardian*,' Grail said. He glanced with expert speed through the stories which Tone had handed him. 'I suppose,' he said, half to himself, 'that we have the enterprising Josiah to thank for these. He must have made himself quite a bob or two.'

' 'Ere, you an' this nutter's not really goin' ter blarst orf at each uvver?' The question was probably intended to be purely rhetorical and to imply loyal rejection of any such crazy possibility, but somehow – perhaps because he was tired after the journey – Tone allowed his inflection to suggest a delicious optimism rather than ridicule.

Grail looked at him coolly and handed back his papers. He gave a quick shake of the head. 'Nutter is right,' he said. 'They're ten deep in these parts. Look, I'll give you a lift in with that projector.'

When the heavier items had been shifted to the house, Tone delved suddenly, as if in response to an afterthought, into one of the door pockets and handed Grail three flat, circular cans. 'Won't be much of a film show wivaht the bladdy film.' He indicated the labels on the cans. ' 'Ere – sorlinarabic.' To this observation he lent emphasis by doing some snake-like dance steps accompanied by a nasal wail.

'See yer in the kasbah!' was Tone's parting sally as he climbed back into the car. The memory of it sustained his spirit all the way to Peterborough.

Birdie had slept late and bathed without haste. She was just coming downstairs when Becket and Lanching joined Grail in the hall, like explorers eager to see the latest batch of provisions from base.

Grail sought out Mrs Patmore and asked if there were a small room in the house which could be darkened for the showing of a film.

'What sort of film?' She looked from one to another with beetling suspicion.

'I don't really see that that matters, so long as the lighting can be controlled,' Grail replied.

'Aye, but . . . I don't think Mr Stamper would like it if . . .' She stared down at the largest package as if expectant of seeing it heave. 'I mean, it won't be something mucky, will it? Mr Stamper wouldn't like that.'

Grail managed to look hurt and stern at the same time. 'Mrs Patmore, really . . .' He turned to Birdie, as if seeking vindication from the most obviously virtuous person present.

Without hesitation, Birdie said goodness me, Mrs Patmore wasn't to worry, the film was just a sort of travel documentary, terribly dull, actually, but all part of a journalist's job, worse luck.

'A gentleman is coming up from London tomorrow or the day after,' added Grail. 'We are just setting this up for him to see and do some translation for us. He is what we call a foreign correspondent.' A benevolent smile, then: 'Just work, Mrs Patmore, just work. Alas.'

The protector of Farmer Stamper's sensibilities finally agreed to their making use of a spare bedroom, at present unfurnished but curtained and with enough space for a small table and a few chairs.

When she had gone back to the kitchen, Becket examined the projector and pronounced it simple enough to use and probably in good order despite its having been, however temporarily, in the charge of Tone.

Grail was opening a large manilla envelope. 'These will be the stills Richardson mentioned. They should make the job of identification a good deal easier.'

Birdie peered over Grail's shoulder as he withdrew a sheaf of prints, enlarged to some ten inches wide. 'Christikins! There's glamour for you.'

The uppermost picture was a head and shoulders shot of a woman in her middle forties. Her eyes were half closed, her mouth, heavily lipsticked, half open. There was a faintly furry rotundity about her features, suggestive of a home life blameless save for over-indulgence in starch.

Grail slid her to the bottom of the pile and revealed a photograph of a much thinner lady, apparently in heated argument with a youngish man wearing a very false moustache. The background also was patently false: it included a pagoda-like structure and a distant battleship. The woman wore a dressing gown; the man a sports blazer and flannels.

'There's a very sophisticated conception of pornography behind all this,' Grail remarked, thoughtfully.

He exposed the next print.

It represented a bedroom scene. There was no one actually on the bed but a woman and a man in police uniform lay beneath it. A second man, wearing dress shirt and dinner jacket but no trousers, was ogling the camera with a sort of lunatic jollity, while a girl attired in a cap and apron stood at his left and rear and made play with a feather duster.

'I must admit I've never gone a bundle on this transvestite thing,' remarked Birdie, after they had silently contemplated the print for some seconds.

Another still showed an encounter inside a hut or shelter between a man in shirt and riding breeches and a girl with a much soiled face and protruding eyes. She was half recumbent on the floor and held an arm protectively across her breasts. The sundry rents in her dress looked to have been rather neatly done. Their effect upon her companion were difficult to judge, as he wore a pith helmet several sizes too big for him. Handfuls of hay lay around and a cab-horse whip stood in one corner.

Lanching, who felt perhaps that it was his turn to provide comment, offered the opinion that it did not seem at first sight to be the kind of material to inflame the baser senses.

'No, no, no – they're selected. I told you. Heavens, you surely don't imagine that just because a film is pornographic there isn't an innocuous shot in it.'

The unexpected sharpness of Grail's retort produced an awkward silence. He broke it himself by sorting off-handedly through the rest of the prints and saying: 'Well, we certainly seem to have a fair selection of participants here for the record. Notice how some of them keep cropping up in different roles, so to speak?'

Birdie had been looking at Grail thoughtfully. She glanced now at Becket. Their eyes held for an instant. Then he forced one of his quick, uncertain laughs.

'Hey, you haven't heard yet, have you, girl?'

She waited, smiling, playing up to him.

Becket nodded his oversized head towards Grail. 'We're losing him.'

'Oh, yes?' Birdie stood, looking from one to another, like a party guest who has missed a joke through leaving the room.

'He is about to be done to death by an outraged mayor.'

'What a way to go!'

There was laughter, Grail's included.

'Not a horse,' said Becket. 'The Mayor of Flaxborough.'

'He's challenged our Clive to a duel,' Lanching added. 'With pistols . . . is that right, Clive?'

Grail shrugged. 'So the more vulgar sections of the Press assert.'

Birdie pressed hands together and parodied girlish hero-worship. 'Oh, blissikins! Hey, may I staunch your wounds? Oh, please!' And she capered up to him and pushed the heel of her hand against his groin.

Suddenly, she was solemn again. She looked round at the others. 'You're not pulling my leg?'

Lanching handed her the *Express*. The story had made the front page, but more than half way down. Birdie wrinkled her nose, then gave Grail a pitying look. 'You poor darling. Below the fold.'

The account began:

Burly Glaswegian Charlie Hockley – His Worship to the 14,482 inhabitants of this quiet little market town – today threw to the floor of his Mayor's Parlour one of the ceremonial white kid gloves that go with his office. The Chief Citizen of Flaxborough was issuing a challenge to a duel – probably the first public 'calling out' in this country for more than a century.

For Mayor Hockley believes that his township has been grossly libelled by a recent article in a Sunday newspaper (not the *Sunday Express*) and considers it his duty on behalf of his fellow citizens to challenge the journalist responsible and demand 'satisfaction'.

Birdie looked up, wonderment on her face. 'This clown must be certifiable. Must be.' She read on.

During the next few days, the man they are calling Honour-bright Charlie here in Flaxborough (motto: In Boldness We Prosper) will await formal apology for statements made in the article of which he complains.

And if the apology is not forthcoming?

'I shall be there – make no mistake about that,' Mayor Hockley told me. 'Of course, the time and place must be secret for the time being. That is tradition, I understand. But I can assure you that all arrangements are being made. I have chosen my second, and what I prefer to call "suitable equipment" is being made available.'

The mayor is widely believed here to have been promised the loan of a pair of authentic duelling pistols together with lessons in their use.

The man named by Mayor Hockley in his challenge, London columnist Clive Grail, was last night not available for comment.

'Weren't you, Clive?' asked Birdie, innocently.

'I shouldn't have thought,' said Lanching, 'that anybody stuck in this part of the world would be available for anything. I'm beginning to feel like a political detainee.'

Becket had been listening with a half smile to the reading and to the remarks of the others. He now looked intently at Grail and said: 'The phone rang yesterday evening at about seven and you answered it. Why didn't you tell us that it was a newspaper man? You knew then about this duel nonsense, didn't you?'

'Of course not. How the hell could I?'

'How could you?' repeated Becket, mockingly. 'Quite simply, old man. This local correspondent – the fellow who's been working up the story – rang up and asked for a quote. And you gave him the old "not available" crap – but not before he'd told you all about it. Oh, come, Clive – it's bloody obvious. Don't treat us like idiots.'

There was silence. The two men – one undersized, aggressive, confident; the other tall, defensive, contemptuous – faced each other across the bowl of scarlet and yellow dahlias that Mrs Patmore had brought in from the garden the day before. Then, as though obeying a cue, both smiled simultaneously and relaxed.

'You're right, of course,' Grail said, lightly. 'It's just that the thing's so ludicrous, so unimportant.'

'Not now, it isn't,' Lanching said. He took the paper from Birdie. 'This mayor bloke may be round the twist, but whoever put him up to this has hit on a pretty effective way of queering our pitch.'

'I don't see that,' said Grail.

'At the least, it's a diversion that he's arranged. At worst, it could win public sympathy and make the *Herald*'s morality campaign look like priggish interference.'

Birdie looked pleased by this suggestion. She reached over and grasped Grail's shoulder. 'There's only one thing for it, darling. You'll have to accept. Tell you what. I'll be your second.'

Grail's impatience flooded back. 'For Christ's sake, stop being such a tit!' He strode to the sitting-room door and slammed it behind him.

The ensuing silence was broken by Becket. 'My, my – we're touchy today. Don't tell me he's publicity-shy.'

'Understandably,' said Birdie. 'When you've shovelled as much shit as dear Clive, a head wind makes you nervous.'

'The office won't like this,' suggested Lanching. 'I wonder they haven't been on to us yet.'

Birdie shook her head. 'Don't you worry – he'll have got in first. Probably last night or first thing this morning. I bet he tried to take personal credit for it.'

'I shouldn't feel very happy,' said Becket with a sort of gloomy relish, 'if a mad mayor was laying for me with a gun. Not round here, I shouldn't. These characters mean what they say.'

Lanching had opened one of the cans of film and was holding a strip up to the light. 'Hot air,' he said, casually. 'It's got to be. If anybody really meant to fight a duel, they'd not advertise it in advance.' He let slip through his fingers another two or three feet of film, frowned dubiously, then wound it back on the reel. 'You might as well,' he said, 'tell the press you're going to commit burglary. Duelling is just as illegal.'

'So is boiling in oil,' observed Becket, 'but that wouldn't deter anybody in Flaxborough, once they'd got into the habit.'

Grail reappeared after about twenty minutes. He looked calm and benevolent. 'I'm going into town for an hour or so,' he announced. 'I'll want you with me, Birdie. Then if Ken and Bob will improvise an Odeon in the meantime, we'll all have an improving movie show when we get back. Right?'

A light drizzle had begun to fall. Grail and the girl hurried across the gravel, the already wet stones slithering away beneath their feet. Grail climbed into the Rolls and leaned across to admit Birdie to the seat beside him. The affability had left his face but his expression was one of anxiety rather than annoyance.

She settled herself into a hunched, half-curled position, indifferent to the expanse of thigh revealed. For a few moments she stared through the rain-stippled windscreen at the stripped harvest field, of whose lines of brown stubble the height of the great car gave a view above the hedge.

Grail, too, was gazing blankly ahead. Becoming aware that he had made no move to switch on the ignition, she looked across at him.

He lowered his eyes and turned the key about in his fingers, as if wondering what it was for.

'Something wrong?'

He remained silent a little longer. Then he said: 'Look, love, I know you're not wildly enamoured of this story . . .'

'Christikins.' The snapped glass of her laugh cut him short. 'Is anybody? Is Bob? Ken? Like hell. It gets worse all the time. Thinner and smellier. You've been conned, boy. And we have to push on because you won't admit it.'

'No,' he said, softly. 'No.' He shook his head. 'You're hopelessly over-simplifying.' The key went home and turned. As the car glided forward, he shook his head again.

The girl seemed to find the mildness of his response puzzling. She watched him carefully, as he guided the car between the green banks of the lane that led them to the main road.

'When you talk of "over-simplifying",' she said, 'I take it that you mean I haven't thought up as many excuses as you have.'

'Excuses for what?'

'For going to town on a story you can't authenticate.'

He gave a short laugh. 'Authentication, dear girl, is in that film you'll see later today. I'm not worried on that score.'

There was a slight pause.

'But you *are* worried,' she said.

'A little, yes. Not for the reasons you suppose.'

'Why, then?'

'I think there are dangers involved that we hadn't reckoned on. Not libel. Nothing like that. More direct. Nastier. Do you see?'

Birdie gazed at him reflectively. The pale, ascetic face, as carefully groomed and cherished as a vain woman's, had lost something of its customary patina of calm self-sufficiency. In particular, his eyes now were alert and nervous.

She spoke with deliberation, still watching him. 'No, darling, I do not see. Tell me more.'

The probe irritated him at once. 'Oh, for God's sake, don't let us get prosaic about this. It's just a feeling I have.'

'Of danger? What kind of danger?'

'Of harm. Of physical harm. To us.'

'To you, you mean.'

'Primarily, dear girl, to me. Naturally. I'm glad you put first things first. But by a supreme effort of selflessness I brought everyone in. The team.' Grail stressed the word so that it sounded silly.

'If you're being serious,' Birdie said, 'I think you should tell me

57

and the others at once exactly why you're so bloody nervous. You get paid for risking martyrdom. We don't.'

They had reached the town's outskirts. In the veil of rain, the big, square, Victorian villas built for the founders of Flaxborough's prosperity loomed amidst their bays and laurels like mourners.

'Where are we going, anyway?' Birdie asked.

'To see your little editor friend. The man who gives you a piece of candy with one hand while he stirs you a mug of hemlock with the other.'

Birdie uncurled and sat upright. 'Oh, come off it, darling. Kebble was very accommodating. He didn't have to be. He's a nice old boy. You leave him alone.'

Grail slowed the car at a junction. 'Where's his beastly little office?'

'I shan't tell you.'

'Look girl: don't try pissing me about, or you'll find yourself out on your little fanny pretty damn quick, and I am not joking, believe me.'

She was shocked not by the words, but by the transfiguration of his face. As he wrenched viciously at the wheel to bring the car into the town-bound traffic stream, the smooth, disdainful features were tightened and sharply lined into an expression of vulgar fury. It was as though a respected statesman had suddenly, in full public view, reverted to his beginnings as party tout and heckler.

Something much more serious, she decided, than Grail's usual pre-revelation nerves was working on his mind this time. Quelling her instinct to counter the abuse, she sulkily gave him directions until the Rolls drew to a halt in the narrow side-street in which was the works entrance to the *Citizen* building.

Mr Kebble rose in a flurry of surprise and delight from his half-acre desk and welcomed Birdie as if she had been Florence Nightingale, making the *Citizen* her very first call on the way back from the Crimea.

Grail had had time to re-compose himself into the image of a distinguished London journalist on a goodwill tour of his lesser dominions. Mr Kebble seized Clive's somewhat limp hand and held it in his own firm, warm grip long enough to impart his sense of the significance of the occasion.

'They tell me,' began the editor, in characteristic acknowledgment of those ubiquitous but anonymous informants who seemed to throng Kebble's Flaxborough like the voices on Prospero's island, 'that you've turned up quite a nice little story here, old chap.'

'As an old newspaper man,' said Clive, graciously, 'you will appreciate its flavour, I think.'

Mr Kebble was peering at both visitors in turn, with a mixture of friendliness and respect. 'Of course,' he conceded, 'we people on the spot are often sitting on a story without knowing it. That does happen, you know.'

Grail waved a spray of white fingers. 'Often a matter of sheer luck, old man. And the nationals do have an unfair advantage in the matter of resources. Take this story, for instance. We were put on to it by our Baghdad office.'

'You don't say, old chap?' Mr Kebble's eyes widened as gratifyingly as if the agency of Haroun al Raschid himself had been claimed.

'Films,' said Grail, airily.

'Ah.' Mr Kebble nodded.

Suddenly, his expression changed to one of anxious solicitude. He leaned closer. 'They tell me old Charlie Hockley has quite flown off the handle. He's the mayor here, you know.'

Birdie gave an inward gasp of admiration for the little editor's bland duplicity. He was, she knew, and Grail knew, the only possible candidate for the authorship of that morning's account in the national press of Mayor Hockley's foray into chivalric fantasy. It was even likely that Kebble it was who had telephoned Grail the previous day for a quote.

'Mind you, old chap,' Kebble went on, kindly, 'you mustn't let Charlie's antics worry you too much. His bark is probably worse than his bite. We must hope so, anyway.'

'Quite a comedian, I gather,' said Clive, having caught something, perhaps, of Mr Kebble's habitual accrediting of information to unnamed sources.

The editor gave a chuckle. It implied that Alderman Hockley's eccentricities had a long and well known history. Birdie found herself searching Grail's face for signs of renewed nervousness.

'I imagine the police are more than capable of dealing with your mayor if he persists in making a fool of himself,' said Grail. Birdie looked away, her guess confirmed. So unimaginative and pompous a retort was not Clive's style. He clearly was rattled.

They heard the thump of one of the outer doors swinging shut. Mr Kebble looked across to the already opening inner door. 'Talk of the devil,' he said softly.

'Hockley?' whispered Birdie, following his glance.

Kebble shook his head. 'Man called Hoole,' he breathed. 'He's Charlie's second.' And he rose to greet the new arrival with an ear-to-ear grin and an arm as eagerly extended as if he had not seen Mr Barrington Hoole in ten long years.

Chapter Seven

'WHAT DOES HE MEAN, "SECOND"?' GRAIL MURMURED TO Birdie. The expansive Mr Kebble sheltered them at that instant from the view of the new arrival and Birdie just had time to pose furtively but very expressively in a representation of taking aim with a pistol before introductions were being made.

Grail's smile for Mr Hoole was as affable as fly-spray. The girl, on the other hand, greeted the optician like a favourite uncle. She hugged his arm and turned to Clive with 'I told you he was a duckikins, didn't I?'

Grail acknowledged this felicitous remark with a slight rise of the lip.

'Mmm . . . ah,' hummed Hoole. 'A fortunate call. For me, at all events. I was not at all sure where to find you, Mr Grail.'

'And why should you wish to find me?' Clive had sufficiently recovered himself to produce his expression of vacant sanctity.

Hoole rubbed his plump little hands and jutted his head forward. He nodded in the friendliest way at Grail and said: 'I have the mmm . . . privilege, sir, of bearing the mayoral commission, as it were. His cartel, as we say in duelling circles. In vulgar speech, challenge. Mr Hockley wants to shoot you. Mmm . . . yes, he does.'

Mr Kebble heard this little address with every appearance of wishing to congratulate both parties. He glanced at each in turn, his face positively pulsating with good humour.

'There now, Clive,' said Birdie. 'You could go further and meet with no nicer invitation.'

Very slowly and deliberately, Grail looked about him, selected a chair, and settled himself into it. He waited some seconds, then said quietly: 'I am not going to spoil an elaborate joke by saying how silly I find all this. Nor shall I insult your intelligence, gentlemen, by pointing out the obvious – namely, that any attempt to carry the joke further would automatically bring those taking part to the notice of the police.'

He gave Hoole, then Kebble, a slow, sad smile, and went on: 'I do not know who you are, Mr Hoole, but you look too old and respectable a tradesman to be mixed up with a . . . a jape of this kind. As for you, Joss – may I call you Joss? – I should like to call upon your journalistic services in a matter much more worthwhile in every sense than this dubious nonsense that somebody has prevailed upon you to promote. Come now – what do you say?'

Only twice during his quarter century of professional practice had Mr Hoole heard himself termed a tradesman. For the rest of that day and during much of the ensuing week he was in a rigor of ice-cold outrage – a condition of which the only detectable symptoms were a persistent small nervous laugh and a white patch in the centre of each of his rosy, tight-skinned cheeks.

Kebble hid his glee behind the frown of earnest interest with which he addressed Grail. 'Anything I can do to help, old chap. Glad to. What exactly had you in mind?'

Grail hitched his chair a little nearer the editor. 'Let me put you in the picture, Joss. I don't think I am betraying any confidences (his glance flicked aside to the optician and back) if I tell you that some film has come into my possession – the *Herald*'s possession, that is. Portrayed in that film are certain people who are residents of this town. It is most important that these people be clearly and accurately identified.'

Grail paused. A drumming noise that had begun quietly with his opening words was now irritatingly obtrusive. Mr Hoole's finger ends were beating upon a resonant desk panel. Grail glared at the offending hand.

'Mmmm . . . if I might just interpose an observation?' said

Hoole. He smiled icily. 'As I mmm . . . intimated before, I do have certain propositions to put to Mr Grail. If he accedes to them, as I hope he will, there will no longer be any need for him to pursue his researches in this area, in which case his requirement of your assistance, Joss, would cease to exist.'

Hoole looked at Birdie, as if in confidence that her common-sense grasp of realities would induce her there and then to declare her alliance with him.

'All right, what *does* His Worship want?' Birdie asked.

'We know that,' said Grail promptly. 'He wants to shoot me. Right, Mr Hoole?'

'Mmm . . . regrettably, yes. But there exist what I believe are termed, in current cant, "options". Perhaps you will permit me to outline them?'

Grail spread a hand in limitless invitation. 'My dear fellow . . .'

'In the first place,' began Mr Hoole, 'my principal – Alderman Hockley – feels that although mmm . . . much damage has been done to the good name of the town by what has already appeared in the mmm . . . the *Sunday Herald* – the *Sunday Herald*? (Yes, said Birdie, that was indeed the name of the paper in question.) Ah, yes . . . he would be prepared to consider honour satisfied if the projected articles were cancelled and a brief apology printed.'

Grail did his best to simulate high amusement. 'Oh, yes? And in the second place?'

'You would undertake to destroy or return to the proper, mmm . . . proper owners, such material in your possession as might be used to discredit the town or its citizens.'

'And do you really imagine,' retorted Grail, 'that this quite unfunny concoction of your mad mayor, or whoever, is going to receive some sort of formal reply?'

Mr Hoole raised a disclaiming hand. 'Ah, you must not regard me as capable of imagining anything, Mr Grail. A second is an absolutely disinterested person, a cypher, one might almost say – a mere carrier of messages.'

'In that case,' said Clive, 'kindly carry this one to your Mr Hockley: Go shoot your own silly brains out and stop wasting other people's time.'

Kebble beamed at Birdie, then, expectantly, at the optician. Hoole, when he chose, could lay tongue to abuse of such refined indecency that it sounded to the uninitiated like a lecture in medical jurisprudence. But on this occasion he merely chuckled and nodded his head four or five times, as if eminently satisfied. Then he left.

'May we now,' said Grail to Kebble, 'get back to the business that brought me here in the first place? This film, Joss. I take it that you won't mind giving us a little help – purely in the matter of identification. The *Herald* does pay rather well, incidentally.'

On the London train that was drawing into Flaxborough Station at that moment, there happened to be three passengers whose first-class tickets bore witness to the generosity of the proprietors of the *Sunday Herald*.

They were, in order of costliness, Sir Arthur Heckington, Queen's Counsel, retained by Herald Newspapers to defend photographer Robert Becket on a charge of aggravated assault with a motor car upon a police officer; Robin Marr-Newton, *Herald* representative in Baghdad, now on leave; and Mr Ben Suffri, of Haringey, an expert upon Islamic languages.

Sir Arthur, who was six feet and four inches tall, wore the full morning rig of a barrister. 'To impress the natives,' he had remarked light-heartedly to Lady Heckington that morning on leaving his Kensington home. The first native to be impressed was the driver of the taxi which he hailed imperiously on emerging from the station. He showed his respect by elaborating a two-hundred yard journey to the offices of Mr Justin Scorpe, solicitor, into a sight-seeing tour of some two and a half miles.

The other two arrivals on *Herald* business were less splendidly attired. They were directed on foot to their immediate destination, the Roebuck Hotel, which was very little further distant than Mr Scorpe's premises. There they registered, and drank some bruise-grey coffee while awaiting transport to Miriam Lodge.

Mr Scorpe received Sir Arthur Heckington with outstretched hand and an 'Ah, Sir Arthur!' so expressive of admiring familiarity that the barrister doubted for a moment his own reasonable conviction that he had never seen this curious looking fellow before in his life.

For Scorpe unquestionably was easily memorable. He was tall, with a big and knobbly skull, and stood poised in well-worn and slightly too large clothes of courtroom black as if he had been hung up, suit and all, from the nape of his scraggy neck. His eyes were dark and deeply set, his nose long, his wide, thin mouth set in a grim smile of forensic omniscience. He carried in his hand a pair of spectacles, plainly too massive to be worn except for very short periods, but without equal in three counties as an instrument of eloquence, when waved; or, when shaken or jabbed, as a weapon of scorn and discomfiture.

'Morning, er, Scorpe,' said Sir Arthur. He spared the wonderful spectacles no more than a brief and quite sour glance. Scorpe put them on and lowered his head so as to peer over their frames, but the barrister was already engaged in his own ritual of clicking open his briefcase and sorting through a thin sheaf of foolscap. Off the spectacles came again. Scorpe grasped them closed, nibbled one side frame, and awaited developments.

Sir Arthur said he would have a word with Scorpe's client before the case came into court again but thought there would be no point in going for anything other than a straight rebuttal.

'Exactly,' said Mr Scorpe, weightily.

'You'll prepare on those lines, then, will you?' said Sir Arthur. He glanced at his watch.

The solicitor looked as if he were about to make a speech, but he got no further than pursing his lips portentously.

'Odd charge,' said Sir Arthur. 'Wouldn't stand up in a thousand years. Police here pretty incompetent, are they?'

A rumble came from the throat of Mr Scorpe. He tapped the furled spectacles against the side of his nose. 'Ah, well . . . as to that, I can but offer . . .'

'I have been given very clearly to understand,' interrupted Sir Arthur, speaking now with greater deliberation, 'that our main object – apart, of course, from demolishing this quite preposterous charge – is to reduce to a minimum the chances of publicity. Don't ask me why; I thought newspapers liked publicity, good bad or whatever.'

Mr Scorpe's lower jaw made movements suggestive of deep cogitation. He spoke. 'The situation as, ah, I understand it, does happen to have . . .'

'Become difficult? Of course. A melodramatic indictment like this was bound to make things difficult to play down. You must keep your witnesses grey, Scorpe, grey. Nothing gaudy, you understand.'

Mr Scorpe hauled a large, cinnamon-tinged handkerchief from an inside pocket, flourished it and began to polish the spectacles, holding them to the light occasionally like a host lifted before a reverent congregation.

'The, ah, chief constable of Flaxborough,' he intoned, 'did, as it happens, communicate by telephone with my clerk no more than, let me see, twenty minutes ago.' He paused to peer at the barrister as if challenging him to interrupt yet again.

Sir Arthur grunted but remained attentive in his fashion, which was by staring sternly through the window at some pigeons circling above the pantiled roof of the opposite building.

'The substance of the chief constable's message, as I am led to believe by what my clerk reported, was to the effect, ah, that the police have decided to offer no evidence upon the charge of assault by motor car. They will, however, or so I gather, proceed summarily with the lesser charge of driving the, ah, said motor car without due care and . . .'

'Attention,' snapped Sir Arthur, with the air of locking Mr Scorpe's verbosity inside a deed box. He consulted his watch once more. 'I do think you might have told me that in the first place, Scorpe. When are they proceeding?'

'It appears that the chief constable holds the view – in deference to my client's professional obligations, of which it seems he has been apprised – that Mr Becket's case might now conveniently be brought to the front of the list and, ah, disposed of . . . just a moment, if you don't mind, Sir Arthur . . .' Scorpe assumed the great spectacles and consulted a sheet of paper on his desk. 'Ah, yes – on Thursday morning at ten of the clock. Subject always' – a crocodile grin – 'to the convenient availability of learned counsel, naturally.'

Sir Arthur nodded and flicked a dust mote from the brim of his bowler with one wash-leather glove. 'Have your clerk fetch a taxi, will you, Scorpe? I'd better go and have a word with this Becket fellow. Then all should be plain sailing, mmm?' And for the very first time since his arrival, Counsel released a tiny, four-guinea smile.

Grail and Miss Clemenceaux had not yet returned when the man from Baghdad and his interpreter were admitted by Mrs Patmore. Convinced by now that 'the newspaper lot' had turned the house into an assembly point for some kind of white slaving conference, the housekeeper stared at both new arrivals with what appeared to be sustained malevolence. In fact, she was trying to memorize their respective features in readiness for helping the Vice Squad with identikit details.

Mr Suffri smiled nervously and said what a pretty hovel and had the corns grown well that year? The housekeeper's only response to this inquiry was to clutch her breast and squeeze past him, and he later confided sadly to Robin Marr-Newton that he feared it was on account of his colour. Mr Marr-Newton, impeccably pink-cheeked and golden-haired son of the titled Foreign Office official whose relationship by marriage to the chairman of Herald Newspapers was Robin's chief, if not solitary, journalistic quali-fication, replied nonsense, there was no racial prejudice these days, he'd even seen wogs in Brook Street, Benny wasn't to worry.

Lanching and Becket were upstairs, assembling the projector in one of the unused bedrooms. The screen had been hung across the only window, effectively blocking out daylight. A collection of several chairs stood outside on the landing. Becket was weav-ing cable in and out of doorways and testing switches.

Marr-Newton introduced himself and his companion, and Lanching made a couple of jokes suitable to the occasion, such as had they brought any dancing girls with them? and would they mind emptying the sand out of their shoes because otherwise Mrs Patmore would have their balls for pincushions.

Some cans of beer were produced and within half an hour a convivial atmosphere prevailed in which stories of Fleet Street coups by Becket and Lanching found exotic counterpoint in Marr-Newton's tales of a foreign correspondent's tribulations in the embassies and ministries of the Middle East, most of which, it appeared, were concerned either with alcohol or venery.

'Have you seen the flick, by the way?' Robin asked eventually.

'Just a few stills,' said Lanching. 'Odd, but tame, I thought.' He turned towards Becket. 'Didn't you think them pretty innocuous, Bob?'

'No,' said Becket. 'Very suggestive.'

Lanching looked at him, uncertain of whether he was being facetious or not. He asked, as a test: 'That one of men dressed as boy scouts, for instance?'

Becket shook his head. 'Boy scouts, nothing. They were supposed to be Mounties. You know – Royal North West Canadian whatsits. Sinister, I thought.'

Robin Marr-Newton had one hand over his face. He was giggling. The others glanced at him.

'Christ! You should hear what the commentator says about that scene. According to him, they're English gentlemen on their way to hunt foxes.'

'Commentator?' Becket was frowning.

Robin shrugged. 'Sort of. In Arabic, of course. Benny here says its incredibly indecent. I thought it hilarious, actually.'

'Do you mean,' said Becket, 'that the film's only *verbally* obscene?' He sounded suddenly concerned, apprehensive almost.

Robin, inclined to answer simply with a guffaw, caught the note in his voice and paused. 'Oh, no,' he said, flatly. 'By no means, duckie.' And he twitched his long, straight, well-bred nose.

Lanching nodded slowly, not looking at him, then said: 'Clive, as you will have gathered, has plunged pretty deeply with this one. I don't want you to think I'm questioning his judgment, or yours – or anybody's, for God's sake – but did he go to town on this strictly on the strength of your say-so? I mean, you were a long way off.'

Marr-Newton frowned. 'I don't quite see what you're getting at, Ken. Long way? Sure, but there are phones, dear lad. One gets asked to chase something up, and one chases. Then all one needs do is produce some money and the job's done. Simple as that. In Baghdad or Biggleswade. Distance no object.'

'You were *asked* to get this film, then?' Lanching sounded surprised.

'Sure. You don't suppose I trog round all the blue picture shows in the Gulf looking for home movies from England, do you?'

Mr Suffri, who had remained silently attentive hitherto, apparently found this notion too funny to be allowed to pass. He grinned at the other three in strict rotation, as if handing round cake, and declared: 'The old red and white and blue more sodding likely, gents!'

Robin gave the interpreter a pat of commendation and said: 'Yes, rather,' to no one in particular. Then, to Lanching: 'The London office was tipped off. Didn't Grail tell you? Who unearthed the original story I don't know, but both Grail and Ricky seemed to think it was someone absolutely reliable. Knew the town, according to Rick. Described details in the film. As I said, I just chased it through the old randy reeler circuit and snaffled a print. The things we do for bloody editors!'

There was a swish of tyres on gravel below the window. Becket moved the screen a little aside and peered down. 'Grail's back.' He stretched to extend his view. 'Somebody else, as well. I think it's a taxi.'

Marr-Newton joined him. They heard voices, one of them plummily imperious. Robin nudged Becket. 'Here comes your own personal legal eagle, old son. My God, the *Herald* must love its children.'

Chapter Eight

'WHAT DO YOU KNOW, SID,' INQUIRED INSPECTOR PUR-BRIGHT of his sergeant, 'about the Flaxborough Camera and Cinematograph Society?'

'I believe Mr Chubb belonged to it at one time,' said Love, putting first things first.

'Indeed? Apart from that, though, should we be aware of anything to its discredit?'

Love considered the question carefully, then shook his head.

Purbright resumed examination of the copy of the *Sunday Herald* which the chief constable, with an air of great gravity, but no comment, had placed on his desk an hour previously.

'It does seem odd,' he said, 'that so blameless an institution seems to appear to this Mr Grail to be some sort of satanic pleasure palace. He promises pretty horrific revelations.'

'Yes, I read it,' declared Love.

Purbright regarded him narrowly. 'Oh?'

'My landlady gets it for her horoscope,' the sergeant explained.

'I only hope,' said Purbright, 'that the planets are more specific than Mr Grail.' He folded and put the paper aside.

Love waited patiently for whatever the inspector had been leading up to. Purbright, he knew very well, did not deliver random questions like a schoolmaster testing the awareness of his pupils.

Purbright rose from his desk and went over to the window. He stared down into the yard where a couple of patrol cars were being hosed.

'The only thing even remotely connected with the cine club that sticks in my mind is the death of that wretched girl who drank developer or something in a darkroom.'

'Edith Bush,' supplied the sergeant, promptly.

'That's the one, yes. Probably absolutely irrelevant. The business just lingers in the memory, that's all. A singularly silly death, as well as wasteful.'

'There was no suggestion of foul play,' Love said. The stiff official phrase was laid before the inspector like a stick retrieved by a youthful, diligent Labrador.

Purbright affected airy scepticism. 'No, there wouldn't be, would there? Old Amblesby was coroner then, remember.'

Love raised his brows and was silent, awed by such worldliness.

'Never mind, Sid.' Purbright turned from the window. 'Some rather more immediate problems have landed on our plate, thanks to these same enterprising guests from Fleet Street.'

'The court case, you mean?'

'Well, that shouldn't give any trouble, now that the chief has trimmed it of Constable Cowdrey's excesses. It goes on as a straight careless driving. Five or ten minutes and no blood spilt. No, I'm thinking of the Charlie Hockley business.'

'Just his fun,' suggested Love, hopefully.

' "Fun" in this context, Sid, is defined at law as either conduct likely to lead to a breach of the Queen's peace, or issuing threats of grievous bodily harm, or conspiring to discharge firearms to the danger of life, or ... oh, I don't know, lots of laughable alternatives of a like kind. Mr Chubb has been reading his *Blackstone* and brooding on all of them.'

'I suppose he wants Alderman Hockley restrained?'

'You could say so, yes.'

Love looked thoughtful, then, quite suddenly, knowing.

'I reckon,' he said, 'that he's being put up to it.'

The inspector mutely invited him to expand his theme.

'Well,' said Love, 'it does seem funny that there should be all this talk about duels just after a pair of duelling pistols was sold by old Knocker Cartwright.'

'You mean he sold them to Charlie?'

'No, to that pal of Mr Kebble's. Little sarky bloke from Chalmsbury. Optician.'

A grin of fond recall spread over Purbright's face. 'Good Lord! Hoole. Barrington Hoole. Remember the Chalmsbury dynamitings, Sid? Barry lost his eye.'

The sergeant frowned. 'He had two when I saw him on Friday.'

'No, not his own eye. It was a bloody great glass model that once hung outside his shop and lit up at night. It used to give people quite a turn if they weren't used to it.'

'I reckon one of those pistols would give someone a turn if it went off,' remarked Love.

Purbright considered. 'I must say those newspaper interviews were suggestive of another hand in the affair,' he said. 'Charlie sounded as if he was working to a script.'

'Kebble's?'

'Could be. But in any case, I shall have to go and see him. No township can tolerate a chief citizen who invites every visitor with a complaint to stand up and be shot.'

Purbright found the mayor in the garden of his home. He was standing at the far end of the lawn, close by the post from which a line of washing was suspended. The mayoress, who had come to the door herself to admit the inspector, was now unpegging some of the clothes and loading them into a big wicker basket. Among them, Purbright noticed, were several heavy woollen vests and a number of pairs of drawers, singularly capacious and of the hue of pease pudding. Mrs Hockley, it seemed, was not of coquettish inclination in the matter of underwear.

His Worship acknowledged with a mere grunt his wife's announcement of 'the inspector of pollis'. He had assumed an awkward-looking sideways stance and was gazing for approval at Mr Hoole, whose plump but trim figure was discernible some twenty yards away against a clump of michaelmas daisies. Mr

Hockley's right arm was raised and he held in his hand a rolled-up newspaper, bent in crude representation of a firearm.

'Better, a little better,' Mr Hoole called out, distance lending his voice an even more nasal quality than usual. 'You ought to be safe against a ball through the heart. Trouble is, your gut profile is a bit mm . . . obtrusive. If he fires low, you could lose the lot.' And Mr Hoole mimed with two hands in a most disconcerting manner the rupture and discharge of a laden abdomen.

Mrs Hockley was scowling at some socks she had just taken down from the line. 'If you don't soon cut your toenails, my lad, you can set about mending these yourself.'

'Och, piss off, woman!' retorted the mayor. She looked re-assured and gave Purbright a smile of understanding before picking up the basket and returning to the house.

The inspector strolled slowly across to Hoole, who hummed and glowed and nodded several times, then averred that it was pleasant to renew acquaintance with a civilized policeman. 'A very rare mm . . . phenomenon, inspector, as you will readily appreciate.'

Purbright said he hoped this good opinion would survive the knowledge of why he, the policeman in question, had called. 'I don't know what the custom is in Chalmsbury, Mr Hoole,' he went on, 'but duels are much frowned upon in this borough. Indeed, they are accounted a most serious breach of the law.'

The optician had been watching his pupil with something less than approval. He now called to him: 'I think we must consider the alternative position of your presenting your rear to the adversary and firing over your left shoulder. It is not without, ah, precedent and it has the advantage of its being difficult to pene-trate the digestive organs from behind. Let us see how you manage.'

Mr Hockley began to lumber about in a circle. His body being far too thick to twist, all he managed in the way of taking aim with his bent newspaper was to stick it under his arm and blindly wave it about.

The optician turned to Purbright with a smile and placed the tips of his fingers together. He seemed pleased to have an excuse to abandon the practicalities of his job as the mayor's second in favour of consideration of its academic aspect.

71

'You may be surprised to learn, inspector,' he said, 'that statistically the chances of being hit are as low as one in six. It is calculated, moreover, that only one man in every fourteen who "go out", as the duelling term is, actually receives the *coup de cœur*.'

Purbright had a fleeting mental picture of fourteen men with pistols trooping forth, rather like the men in the song who went to mow a meadow. 'It is still against the law, Mr Hoole,' he murmured, 'however small a proportion of casualties proves fatal.'

The spectacle of the suspended vests had caught Mr Hoole's eye. He frowned and called out to the mayor: 'Are those mm . . . garments on the line yours? Those which look like knitted shrouds.'

Mr Hockley abandoned his attempt to squint over his left shoulder and looked in the direction indicated by Hoole.

'Those are vests, laddie. Of course they're mine. Why else do you think I've never ailed anything?'

His second made a face expressive of the utmost disapproval. 'Never, never, my dear sir, fight a duel with wool next to the skin. The ball will carry half a yard of the wretched stuff into the wound.'

Purbright, while aware that his authority was being disgracefully flouted by the calm continuation of this illicit training session, was strongly tempted to satisfy his personal curiosity on certain points.

'Hence, I presume,' he said to Hoole, with reference to the optician's assertion, 'the loose silk shirts one sees in pictures of duels. They were not favoured simply on account of their romantic aspect?'

'Indeed, no,' declared the expert. 'A severely practical precaution. And the looser the shirt, of course, the more difficult for one's adversary accurately to delineate his target.'

'Ah,' said the inspector, pleasantly enough to encourage Mr Hoole to distil further wisdom.

'I personally tend,' Hoole continued, 'to the view of the Bois de Boulogne school. It always favoured the tight, black, high-collared morning coat as presenting the narrowest target possible and the most difficult to sight against a dark background, such as a wood.'

The mayor was showing signs of finding these refinements tiresomely irrelevant to the task in hand. He came up and clapped his second and the inspector on the shoulder and said something about a wee dram.

'One hears,' said Purbright to Hoole, on the way back to the house, 'references to "paces" in duelling. At what distance do they . . . did they, rather . . . actually fire at each other?'

'Mmm . . . paces, yes. Ah, well, anything from ten to fourteen paces will answer. A pace being three feet. The poorer one's marksmanship, the shorter a distance one should choose. Naturally.'

'Naturally,' echoed Purbright.

'That dratted scribbler,' put in Mr Hockley, with devastating contempt, 'can choose half a mile, gentlemen. Half a mile. I'm telling you. And listen – I'll still make him wish he'd never set foot in this little old bailiwick, believe me!' And he blew into the paper barrel of his proxy pistol as zestfully as a moss trooper.

In the mayor's parlour, whisky and glasses had been placed in readiness – presumably by Mrs Hockley, for a thick woollen sock had been stretched sacrilegiously over the bottle. The mayor whipped it off, looked about him irresolutely for a moment, then stuffed the sock into a jar of candied fruits, lately presented to his lady by Gosby Vale Women's Institute. The bottle he rubbed hastily with his sleeve before unscrewing the cap and sluicing a generous measure of Glenmochrie into the three tumblers.

Mr Hockley raised his own drink. 'Powder and blood!'

Not even his abettor found himself able to respond to this ferocious toast. Mr Hoole murmured diffidently and took the tiniest of token sips at his liquor. For the inspector, it clearly was time to make an unequivocal statement of policy. Sadly, he moved his drink a little aside – into reserve, as it were – and addressed the mayor.

'I'm sorry, Mr Alderman, but this really must not go any further. You know perfectly well – as does Mr Hoole here – that what you propose, or pretend to be proposing, is against the law. Neither the chief constable nor I believe that you have any intention to harm Mr Grail. We appreciate that you are making a gesture – a dramatic gesture – in pursuance of genuinely held principles. But it must stop at that. Now, then, Mr Mayor, if you will give me your assurance to that effect, we can enjoy this friendly drink and go our ways. What do you say, sir?'

For some moments, the mayor appeared to be considering Purbright's proposition with great solemnity. The inspector, who had been slightly taken aback by his own eloquence, awaited a sign that he might now drink his Glenmochrie with an easy conscience. Mr Hoole said nothing, but continued to smile at his fingers as if they were a class of favourite pupils who had just been subjected to a nonsensical disquisition by a visiting lecturer whom he would shortly discredit.

Mr Hockley, dark with resolution, champed portentously several times and then said: 'Aye, I realize that you're doing what you consider your duty, inspector, but there's something that I don't think *you* realize. The whole town's up in arms over this *Sunday Herald* business. I tell you, I've not known anything like it in all my years on the council. Hey' – he jabbed the mayoress's favourite coffee table so hard with his forefinger that whisky from Purbright's glass jetted forth and began to dissolve its surface polish – 'do you know that my telephone has scarcely stopped ringing since yesterday morning? It's the truth that I'm telling you: the whole town . . .'

Purbright held up his hand. 'Mr Mayor, I am not contesting that the article in the paper has caused resentment. You may well feel that your official position obliges you to lend a voice to that resentment. But this is not a frontier town in nineteenth-century America, Mr Mayor, and you are not a sheriff. If Flaxborough can be said to have such a person, I suppose it's me. So now let us have no more talk of shooting people. Agreed?'

Mr Hockley shook his head so vehemently that Purbright fancied he could hear his jowls flapping.

'Never!' the mayor declared, and downed his whisky in one. 'This has got to go forward to a finish. You can lock me up if you like, inspector' (the thought of so outlandish and embarrassing an expedient had never entered Purbright's head) 'but you cannot stop the ratepayers knowing the truth.' Suddenly he looked slyly pleased with himself. The television people, he confided, were coming along that very afternoon to interview him.

Oh, Christ, the inspector reflected, they bloody would be, wouldn't they. There would be no holding this maniacal Rob Roy now. He glanced in despair at the optician. Mr Hoole's pince-nez were reflecting light in such a way that it could not be determined whether his eyes were open or closed. But there was no mistaking his smile.

'Good day, gentlemen.' Purbright had risen and half turned away. He felt a little like the visitor to a closed ward in a psychiatric hospital who notices for the first time that none of the doors has a handle on the inside.

Mr Chubb received the inspector's report in gloomy silence. Then, 'I feared as much,' he said, which was not strictly true because he had not previously given the matter enough thought to feel anything more than mild curiosity.

'We could seek a court injunction, sir.'

'Against our own mayor, Mr Purbright? Oh, come now. There has been enough dreadful publicity already without our inviting more.'

Purbright pursed his lips and rubbed the side of his nose. 'Judge in chambers?'

The chief constable shook his head. 'The trouble with this chap Hockley is that he sees grievances everywhere. Very Scottish, you know. They haven't our capacity to reach reasonable settlements.'

'Do I take it, then, sir, that we are to remain officially neutral? The position might be difficult to justify subsequently if somebody does actually get hurt.'

Mr Chubb gestured impatiently. He, too, had been finding the presence of the London journalists an abrasive impurity in the stream of Flaxborough life. But almost immediately he mustered a things-could-be-worse smile for his inspector's benefit.

'Look at it this way, Mr Purbright,' he said. 'We all are well aware that a duel is illegal. But what about half a duel? The law says nothing about that. And as long as this London newspaper fellow treats poor old Hockley's challenge as a bit of nonsense and doesn't do anything mad, such as turning up with a pistol or a sword himself, I really cannot see that there is any call for us to get involved.'

'Just as you say, sir.' Purbright turned to leave.

For several minutes, Mr Chubb remained standing by the fireplace in his office, that vantage point from which he customarily listened to the representations of his officers, rather in the manner of a Roman patrician, poised against a pillar. On this occasion, though, he was less than happy with the interview's outcome, despite understandable pride in his spontaneous production of the 'half a duel' concept. For if there was one thing calculated to disturb the chief constable more than another, it was prompt and unqualified agreement with one of his opinions by Inspector Purbright. Something, Mr Chubb felt, was going to happen. Something against sharing responsibility for which he had failed adequately to insure himself. Something pretty awful.

Chapter Nine

THE FILM THAT WAS RECEIVING WHAT KELVIN PRILE sardonically termed its Flaxborough première was entitled, according to Mr Suffri, *Within the Bedchambers of British Persons of High Connection*. How he contrived so elaborate a translation of the small serpentine cypher on the lids of the containers, no one else present was sufficiently knowledgeable to question, but Sir Arthur Heckington subjected the interpreter to one of his most challenging courtroom scowls without causing him to amend a single syllable.

The barrister, whose interview with Becket had been of no more than eighty or ninety guineas' duration, readily accepted Grail's invitation to watch the film. There was, after all, nothing else to do before dinner, which he preferred to take late. Moreover, he sensed a certain anxiety in the party. Splendid. Sir Arthur liked anxiety, particularly in publishing circles. Nothing on earth was more lucrative than a leading brief for the defence of a newspaper in a libel case.

'Bit near the knuckle, Grail, eh?' he inquired jocularly as the company settled into its assortment of chairs to face the screen. He sounded almost indecently sanguine.

Becket was projectionist. In the less familiar role of sound engineer, he had encountered some difficulties but these –

associated mainly, he said, with the fact that the voices had been superimposed in what he took to be Arabic – were now overcome.

Close beside him sat Mr Suffri. His instructions were to provide, as well as he was able, a simultaneous rendering of the sound-track into English. If Mr Suffri's unquenchable smile was anything to go by, smooth achievement was assured.

Grail and the barrister were flanked by Mr Kebble and Birdie Clemenceaux. Birdie, to Mr Kebble's surprise, was wearing spectacles for the occasion; they imparted an alert and business-like quality that he had not seen before.

In the front of the group sat Lanching, Marr-Newton and Prile. Prile's presence had been counselled by Kebble, who said that he himself could claim only a few months' close acquaintance with Flaxborough society. Prile, on the other hand, had been on the staff of the *Citizen* since shortly after the death of Marcus Gwill, its one-time proprietor of notorious memory, and there was not a face in the town which the chief reporter could not identify. ('Give him a stool, not a comfortable chair,' Mr Kebble had thought fit to add confidentially, but without explicit reference to Mr Prile's remarkable propensity for going into trance.)

On a signal from Becket, Lanching reached across to the wall and switched off the light. In contrast, the succeeding gloom seemed absolute. Silence, too, was complete for some seconds. Then somebody booed, facetiously; it was generally thought to be Prile, who had not come along with very good grace. 'We want our money back,' Birdie called out. Secretly listening outside the door, Mrs Patmore curled a lip derisively. Them and their mucky pictures: like a lot of kids.

At last the projector whirred suddenly into action and the screen became a rectangle of pulsing white light. There arose a smattering of ironic applause. The white rectangle acquired a decorative border of complicated geometric designs. Within this border, a couple of lines of script appeared. The voice of Mr Suffri, loud and very pleased with itself, was heard in the land.

'If you are prepared, everybody, adventure one, the Warm Encounter of a Sea-going Gentleman!'

The first scene appeared on the screen. It seemed to be of a maritime nature: a quayside, perhaps, or part of a foreshore. There certainly was a ship of some kind in the distance. The camera closed in upon two figures. One was a woman. She appeared to be wearing a dressing. gown. Her companion, who wore naval uniform, looked younger, although he had a substantial moustache. A voice, speaking a language unintelligible to everyone present but Mr Suffri and, questionably, Marr-Newton, emerged from the amplifier. Within seconds, it was being accompanied by the joyous tones of the interpreter, determined to reduce translation lag to zero.

'It is being expounded here,' shouted Mr Suffri, 'that the gentleman before us is a British navy officer of high family who departs upon a battleship to seize oil wells without success. The lady is his lady and she is related to the Earl of somewhere my ear fails to determine.'

Prile had turned round and was whispering to Mr Kebble, who seemed much intrigued by whatever the chief reporter had imparted to him.

The explanatory voice ceased. There followed a development so odd that most of the audience supposed something to have gone wrong with the sound track.

The characters on the screen now presented the appearance of speaking to each other very slowly indeed, while making the most extravagant gestures. And yet their voices chatted on in a conversational world of their own. Birdie caught Grail's eye and grimaced her unbelief.

Mr Suffri, utterly indifferent, it seemed, to such discrepancies, enthusiastically pursued his role.

'The lady say the gent is resembling to a horse . . . ah . . . yes, a horse for fights. A fight horse, you know? And the gent makes answer he is burning with conflict. And now something I regret I must not translate, but it is most shocking for polite people you understand. And there is more of like nature. A moment, please. Ah . . . Ah, yes. I can maybe translate that one. He say he cannot wait to take ownership of her uncompared orbs (it is her chest is indicated, I do not have to tell you). And she replies, all, all, have it all, this day the manservant and maidservant at my hubby's hall are granted leave, come you marauding steed.'

The scene changed. In the background now was the facade of the Oddfellows Hall, Flaxborough. A group of a dozen or so people stood facing the camera. They appeared cheerful and imbued with a sense of occasion. In the centre of the group, the two characters from the previous scene held hands and posed and giggled a good deal. She had exchanged her dressing gown for skirt and cardigan. He had jettisoned his moustache, but was still wearing the uniform jacket.

The voice of the commentator was back. Mr Suffri, close behind it, sounded like a guide with a megaphone. 'Here have we the British officer of high family with the lady already referenced and some more of British society notably two esquires of Berkshire. Assignations are being hammered up but the secret camera lens catches the truth.'

Prile and Mr Kebble were now conferring quite animatedly. Names were being jotted down between glances at the screen.

A visual announcement within one of the heavily decorative borders that seemed a stock feature of this kind of entertainment proclaimed, according to Mr Suffri, that the ensuing events had been 'captivated with private lenses within the lounging room of the Earl's how-you-say, too hungry, not satiable – relative by marriage.'

It took the audience some time to discern anything at all in the picture of a large, shadowy chamber, of indeterminate height and breadth, whose walls – if walls it had – were draped in dark sheeting. There were no windows, no doors. It was devoid of anything in the way of conventional decoration or furnishing – or so it seemed in what little illumination there was. This, one realized after a while, derived from a single shaft of light from above that passed out of camera shot at the bottom left-hand corner of the screen.

Then movement became noticeable. Two figures – at first merely shadows against shadows – had entered from the right. They crossed slowly into centre screen.

The figures approached the fixed, transverse spotlight. It caught the forearm of one of them. Braid glinted brilliantly at the cuff.

'Ah, the naval officer of high family,' murmured Birdie to Sir Arthur. He sniffed good-naturedly, flattered.

A section of the second figure moved across the shaft of light. Folds of a silken garment, flowered in pink and blue, parting a little to disclose a knee.

79

The lady of aristocratic connections, clearly, back in her dressing gown.

The figures began to move back and forth in tandem. A clinch had developed. The next time the woman's knee came into view, the gown had parted a lot more and the hand sleeved in gold braid was lending it such resolute assistance that most of one thigh and part of the other were disclosed.

Birdie nudged Sir Arthur's arm. 'Is he a captain or just first mate?' she whispered. 'I never know how many rings mean what.'

Sir Arthur, who had done a little yachting in his time, replied indulgently that his reading of the decoration put the man down as commodore.

Some wrestling was now going on. By judicious and, it had to be admitted, quite artistic manoeuvring, the pair were executing a sort of mutual striptease in such a manner that a limited additional area of nudity was exposed by each with every pass into the light beam.

The incredible dubbed voices returned. This time, some attempt had been made to give an impression of urgent desire. The result, unfortunately, was more suggestive of argument between a pair of falsetto-voiced taxi drivers. Mr Suffri nevertheless was ready to do his best.

'The gentleman,' he bawled, 'says he intends to pulverize the lady in the pistol and mortar of his lusting and she gives answer which please I wish to be excused. Now the gentleman makes words difficult to understand in English but readily to be significant in my country of the making love of leopards – thus, grurrh, grurrh. I hope that is carried to you gentlemen and lady.'

Birdie leaned back in her chair and craned past Sir Arthur's back towards Grail. He was far too preoccupied to notice, and when, helplessly impelled by pure mischievousness, she growled loudly into his ear, he was so startled that he leaped sideways into collision with poor Mr Kebble.

'Oh, Christikins! I'm sorry,' said Miss Clemenceaux, with absolute sincerity. She had, even in the moment of succumbing to temptation, seen in Grail's face something not of disgust; not, certainly, of sexual excitement; but of sheer, unalloyed fright. And she thought she knew why.

80

The two protagonists on the screen had succeeded by now in divesting each other of every article of clothing and were embracing in a kind of erotic ballet in and out of the spotlight. Although the camera had been gradually bringing them into much closer range revelation was solely of limbs and torsos: not once was the face of either allowed to reflect enough light to betray identifiable features.

At this point, the scene was obliterated with startling suddenness by another bordered announcement.

Mr Suffri obliged. 'The gallant Sir and beloved make pause for refreshing.'

To the evident astonishment of Prile, who again turned and entered into urgent colloquy with his editor, there appeared next on the screen the representation of a number of people dining at a long table. The naval character was now respectably attired, not in uniform but in dress shirt and dinner jacket. His companion in earlier scenes was also present, but at a distance of four or five places and closely conversing with a man of about her own age.

In the centre of the group was a quarrelsome-looking man with restless, red-rimmed eyes and a small moustache. Around his shoulders was the heavy, elaborately-fashioned gold chain of office of a mayor of Flaxborough.

Commentary resumed. 'Here we see feasting of aristocratic citizens who prepare for more love encounterings,' declared the faithful translator at the top of his voice. 'The lord mayor of this county is taken prisoner by our private camera as he makes wagers upon the longlastingness of his sporting chaps.'

Another title abruptly blacked out the festivities at the moment of the mayor's beginning to rise ponderously to his feet, presumably to propose a toast.

'Thus our hungry lady is strongly astounded,' Mr Suffri supplied.

Action was transferred once again to the draped chamber. The sudden changes of scene were making one characteristic of the film obvious: the footage that featured the leading participants against this background of curtain-like obscurity was more steadily registered and in better focus than the rest.

The audience was beginning to show a little restiveness. It

reflected embarrassment as much as boredom, for the imminence of the first of whatever series of erotic climaxes were contained in three reels of film had been sensed by everyone except, perhaps, the dedicated Mr Suffri.

After some minutes more of the nude arabesques in and out of the spotlight, the camera moved down and along the slanting beam to reveal what lay on the floor within the oval pool of illumination at its end.

The audience saw a pile of loosely coiled rope that looked thick enough to moor a shrimping boat; beside it lay a telescope and a light fisherman's anchor.

'The mind,' confided Birdie to Sir Arthur, 'boggles.'

Leaning towards her sympathetically, he half rose from his seat. 'I'm sure your colleagues don't expect you to subject yourself to any more of this,' he whispered. 'Perhaps you'd like me to, ah . . .'

Birdie rejected the half-formulated offer of safe conduct to more salubrious surroundings with a shake of the head and a brave smile. 'My job, duckie,' she said carelessly, patting his extended hand.

Sir Arthur sat down again. *Plucky girl*, he told himself, then settled, not entirely without pleasurable anticipation, to resume his watching brief.

What followed in the next ten minutes or so was to impress indelibly upon the minds of everyone present (Mr Suffri, possibly, excepted) associations so bizarre and powerful that none was able ever again to glimpse a loop of rope, let alone a telescope or an anchor, without suffering a brief attack of breathlessness.

The culmination of these extraordinary events coincided with the end of the reel. Becket called for lights. There was much blinking, stretching and puffing of cheeks.

'Christ!' somebody commented.

'Well, I neverkins!' added Birdie, wide-eyed.

'I should hope not either,' murmured Queen's Counsel. By force of habit, he looked about him for a brief, then, having failed to find one, stared sternly at Grail and shook his head.

Grail was pale with shock and anger. Ignoring Sir Arthur, he sought and confronted Robin Marr-Newton.

Robin had every appearance of being pleased with himself. He grinned at Clive in the manner of a car salesman after an impressive test drive.

'Well, squire? How's that for starters? I must say there's some unexpected talent in the rural outback of the old country.'

'You bloody, half-baked, misbegotten . . .'

Grail's mouth made a few more movements without the emission of sound. Then he ran his fingers through his hair, clutched the back of his neck for a moment in impotent fury, and turned away.

Mr Kebble was watching him with his usual chubby-faced benignity, but there was speculation – puzzlement, even – in his eyes. He rolled a pencil up and down between his palms. Grail could hear it clicking against the editor's rings. 'Oh, for f . . .' He controlled himself, swallowed, and managed a weak smile for the joint benefit of Mr Kebble and Prile, who was about to show the editor something he had written in his notebook.

'Do we want to see any more of this stuff?' Becket asked the company at large.

There were non-committal murmurs. Several heads turned towards Grail, master of ceremonies. 'Hang on a minute,' he said, and moved his chair close to Kebble's.

'Bit odd, all this, isn't it, old chap?' the editor said to him. 'Poor Kelvin here's just about buggered and bewildered. Tell him, Kelvin.'

The chief reporter of the *Citizen* turned sad and heavy-lidded eyes to Grail, then to his notes.

'I'd better go through it in order,' he said. 'You remember that first scene – the bloke and the woman singing. Well, that . . .'

'Singing?' Grail challenged.

'Oh, yes. That's what they were doing, actually. The sound track with those weird jabbery voices had obviously been added later. What we saw was part of a stage show. Flaxborough Amateur Operatic Society. *Madame Butterfly*, what else?'

God, of course – the dressing gown, a prop kimono . . . and that unlikely naval uniform – US Navy Lieutenant Pinkerton.

'Ages ago,' said Prile. 'It was when I first came here. I'm not sure of the woman's name, but I think it was Cannon. She was female lead for years after her voice had gone. The fellow I certainly do recognize. One of Flax's more notorious sons. Brian Periam.'

Grail nodded impatiently, as if names now were the least of his concerns. Mr Kebble raised his brows. 'Identification *was* what you wanted, old chap? Kelvin has quite a list. The woman we can check later.'

'Who would have made that film of the opera?' Grail asked.

'Oh, somebody in the Cine Club,' Prile replied. 'They've compiled quite a record of local do's over the years. That shot of the crowd outside the Oddfellows Hall was done probably in the early sixties. Operatic Society again. It used to have an annual outing.'

Birdie had joined them. 'What about that dinner?' she asked.

'The Operatic,' confirmed Prile. 'At the Roebuck, by the look of it. Pointer was mayor that year – the bloke who looked a bit like Hitler. Dead now.'

'One thing's for sure, Mr Kebble,' said Birdie. 'Flaxborough must be the only town in England that requires its amateur opera singers to be Khama Sutra specialists.'

Kebble chuckled with gratification. 'We don't do badly for a little place,' he said.

Behind her smile, Birdie was watching carefully the editor and Prile in turn. Both betrayed awareness of something grossly at odds with probability, something that each was content to leave for interfering London journalists to worry about.

Grail put a final question to Kebble and Prile.

'Did you notice anything about the setting of the actual sex business to indicate where it could have been staged? Anywhere round here, I mean?'

Both newspapermen looked dubious. 'No idea,' said Kebble. 'Could have been anywhere fairly spacious.'

'The light wasn't much help,' Prile said.

'Nor were those sheets or curtains, or whatever they were, in the background,' added Mr Kebble. 'As a matter of fact, they rather put me in mind of a studio.'

Grail's mouth tightened. He had received exactly the same impression. And it had contributed in no small degree to his present feeling of dismay.

Chapter Ten

IN FURTHERANCE OF HIS CLAIM TO BE AN OCULIST AND
not an optician, Mr Barrington Hoole never opened his consulting
rooms before ten o'clock in the morning. Sometimes it was nearly
eleven before he arrived, but it did not matter, for latter-day
prosperity enabled him to employ a receptionist sufficiently well
educated to intimidate such of his clients who might object to
being kept waiting. On Saturdays and Mondays, his premises
remained closed altogether. Such elusiveness had so enormously
increased Mr Hoole's professional reputation, that the days when
he 'kept a shop, and 'sold glasses' were eclipsed.

He had ample time, therefore, to break his journey back to
Chalmsbury on the Tuesday morning, in order to call upon Clive
Grail and formally to tell him that his rejection of the Mayor of
Flaxborough's challenge could not be accepted as the act of a
gentleman and that the preparations of the aggrieved party would
proceed forthwith.

Grail heard him out with an expression of gloomy indifference,
then wandered from the room after instructing the only other
person present – who happened to be Mrs Lily Patmore – to
'throw the pompous little lunatic into the road.'

The housekeeper looked shocked. She appealed to Mr Hoole,
whom she believed to be a doctor of sorts, and therefore vener-
able, not to take too much notice of the gentleman. He was, she
explained, not quite himself that morning, having spent the
previous afternoon watching some sort of a picture show in a
darkened bedroom which had upset him and little wonder.

'Mmmm . . .' hummed Mr Hoole, and went his ways.

Mrs Patmore noticed that Grail's air of glum abstraction did not
lift. The rest of the London party also appeared thoughtful and
depressed. Perhaps they were worried about this ridiculous duel,
or whatever it was. She smiled grimly to herself, having thought
up a little anatomical joke about shooting low.

At about eleven o'clock, Grail left the house after telling the
housekeeper not to include him in her arrangements for lunch, as
he proposed to go for a long walk on his own in order to combat

a headache which had persisted since the night before. It had been suggested to him, he said, that Gosby Vale was a pleasant spot and that good scenery was to be enjoyed between there and a place called Mudlum or something.

'Moldham,' Mrs Patmore corrected. 'Moldham Meres is nice.'

'Yes, I'm sure Moldham Meres is very nice. Or should I say *are*?'

And those, Mrs Patmore was to inform Inspector Purbright later, were the very last words the poor gentlemen said. By then, they had been invested with solemnity, if not significance, by subsequent events. When actually uttered, though, they struck her as just another instance of London sarcasm, and as soon as Grail had turned and taken the first step of his walk she stuck out her tongue at his back and slammed the door.

The others hung about as they generally did, reading papers and having drinks from time to time, and writing things and then screwing them up, and wandering from room to room, and scratching themselves, and making telephone calls, and opening packets of biscuits, and then forgetting where they had put them, and reading more papers, and using vases and cups and sherry glasses as ashtrays.

Mrs Patmore wore her disapproval of these shiftless habits like an enveloping black cloak. It had no effect. None of the unwanted guests seemed to be aware of her. She marched upstairs, fumed in solitude in her bedroom for half an hour, then quit the house in time to catch the noon bus into town. It wouldn't hurt that lot to get their own dinner for once. And if Bert Stamper didn't like it, he knew what he could do.

'Thank God for that: the old crow's pissed off at last.'

Mrs Patmore had been in error. Her presence had not been ignored, and Becket's announcement from his vantage point at one of the front windows produced immediate response from his two colleagues.

Lanching went to the staircase. 'I'll make sure that that room's got enough stuff in it.'

'Bedclothes,' Birdie called to him. 'Don't forget them. And check the lock and the key. Oh, and you'd better take a look round and see if there's a pot anywhere.'

'A what?' Lanching was leaning over the banisters, puzzled.

'A pot, for God's sake. Chamber. They do exist, you know. And try thinking in terms of siege tactics. OK?'

Lanching shrugged and went up the rest of the stairs.

Birdie turned to Becket. 'Bob, you keep an eye open for Louring Lil coming back. It shouldn't be for an hour or two, with any luck.'

'How long are *you* going to be?' Becket asked. His bearing seemed more lively than Lanching's. The sulkiness that had characterized most of his behaviour since the group's arrival in Flaxborough was no longer in evidence. The big head was set at a pert angle, challenging – almost derisory. *You're enjoying yourself, my lad*, Birdie thought to herself.

Aloud she said: 'Twenty minutes. Maybe half an hour. Unless he's cocked things up.'

Becket grimaced. '*That* wouldn't surprise me.'

'I'll bring the car round the back. Make sure the kitchen door isn't locked. And if dear Lily does turn up again, you'd better stand outside to give me plenty of warning.'

Birdie left at once. At the end of the lane, she was about to turn in the direction of Pennick and Gosby when she noticed Mrs Patmore standing at the bus stop on the other side of the road. After brief consideration, she drove over and drew to a halt beside her.

'I'm just going into town; can I give you a lift?'

It was not an offer which even Mrs Patmore, still rigid with resentment of Goings On, could refuse.

'A bit of shopping,' Birdie explained as they glided silently through the Flaxborough approaches. It was as well to be remembered as having made an excursion in a direction opposite to that taken by Clive.

She set Mrs Patmore down near the Corn Exchange, crossed the further side of the Market Place and doubled back over the bridge, leaving the town by Burton Place and Heston Lane. There would be a back road in a couple of miles or so, if she remembered that morning's map-reading correctly, that would take her through a place called something-Willows and on to North Gosby.

There was, and it did.

At North Gosby, Birdie stopped and examined the map for the

last time. The references were clear enough, and quite simple. She drove on.

The derelict railway station that once had served the little village of Hambourne was reached by a short paved incline leading from the main road. Grass already was growing through the cracked concrete surface and several small bushes had established themselves around the entrance to what had been the booking office.

Up the incline Birdie backed the Rolls, after ensuring that no other traffic was in sight. Once off the road, the car was effectively screened from view by an overgrown hedge and a grove of elders. A concourse of small birds that had been stripping the trees of their dark loads of berries burst upward in a noisy cloud.

A face peered cautiously past a corner of one of the glass-less windows. Birdie raised a hand. She took the car as close to the doorway as she could.

Grail, looking pale, untidy and rather tired, emerged with almost melodramatic furtiveness and made a grab for the rear door.

Birdie resisted an impulse to laugh. 'It's all right,' she said, 'we're in the middle of bloody nowhere here. Take your time.' She twisted round in her seat and pulled aside a heavy travelling rug as Grail got in the car and tried awkwardly to squat out of sight. 'All right, take your time,' she said again. 'There's tons of room and the floor's moderately clean. Lie flat and pull this over you.' She let the rug fall across his knee.

'There were snakes in that dreadful place.'

Birdie let in the clutch. 'How fascinating. It must be quite a little nature reserve.'

'You've been the hell of a time.'

'Oh, ballsikins. You're lucky to have got away so quickly. It was solely out of consideration for you that we decided to pick you up in daylight. It's bloody risky.'

At the junction, she held the car back in the shelter of the greenery until the road was empty in both directions. Then she put it swiftly on the way back to Flaxborough.

The plaintive voice rose once more from beneath the rug. 'There'll be hell to pay if this crazy scheme goes adrift.'

'It won't have to, then, will it?' The girl was watching for cars in her rear mirror. Oncoming drivers – and there were very few at this time of day – went by too quickly to be of much account as potential witnesses; one intent on overtaking, though, would be far more likely to memorize details.

'What was bothering me,' said the rug, 'in that awful hideout – apart from snakes and rats – was a pronounced doubt of how reliable those other two are. Why should they take this kind of a risk on my account?'

'Why should I, for that matter?'

There was silence for a while, then: 'Because you wouldn't like getting the chop any more than I should, and our necks would be side by side, believe me.'

They passed through Pennick village. After another half mile, Birdie began to watch for a silo on the right-hand side that served as a guide to the opening of the lane to Stamper's house. There it was. She braked, swung the car sharply at right angles, and within a few seconds it was safely among trees. They had passed only four vehicles during the whole journey from Hambourne.

They entered the house by the kitchen door. Grail, still inclined to extravagant secretiveness, scuttled inside with the rug over his head. He looked like a prisoner on a multiple rape charge, dodging Press cameras.

He threw himself into an armchair in the sitting room, winced as if in memory of protracted suffering, and said something about a drink for Christ's sake.

Lanching stood by, frowning anxiously. 'Shouldn't he be in his room? It's all ready.' He glanced at the window. 'Somebody's only to look in . . .'

Becket entered with gin and tumblers. He had the calmly sanguine expression that he had worn ever since that conference in the early hours at which desperate measures had been propounded to deal with a desperate situation.

Grail seized his drink and swallowed half of it at once. 'I was hours in that damn place. What are we doing about lunch?'

Before anyone could offer an answer, Grail was bent forward, frantically massaging an ankle with his free hand. 'One of those bloody things bit me,' he declared. Some gin splashed from his agitated glass.

'Ken's perfectly right,' said Birdie. 'You're going to have to go up to that room now and stick there. Lock it and keep it locked.

Boring as hellikins, and all that, we know. But it's the only safe way. One little slip and the thing blows up in our face.'

'I get claustrophobia,' complained Grail. He drank what remained of his gin.

'Hard luck.' Birdie stood over him, waiting. With great show of pain and reluctance, he struggled to his feet. He beckoned to be handed the bottle. Lanching gave it to him. 'Come on.' Birdie led the way out of the room.

When they reassembled, minus Grail, it still was the girl who seemed to be the organizer. She looked at her watch. 'When do we start showing anxiety about the poor man?'

Becket pointed out that there was no one around for them to show anxiety *to*.

'Mrs Whatsit will be back before long,' Birdie replied.

'She'll do for now. Then I'm hoping the office will ring during the evening. Richardson has a head start over the entire human race when it comes to worrying.'

'What happens,' asked Lanching, 'if London wants us to call in the police?'

Birdie smiled wrily. 'In that case, the phone will have to ring just as we are about to summon the constabulary and, lo, we shall hear the disguised voice of one of poor Clive's captors. I originally thought that one o'clock in the morning would be a good time for a ransom demand, but if we're pushed, we shall simply have to bring it forward a bit.'

Becket was rummaging in a sideboard cupboard. He produced a couple of cans of beer.

'Even so,' he said, 'the office could still insist on the police being told.'

Birdie handed him her tumbler. She shook her head. 'Not if we make the threat sound bloodthirsty enough. The saintly Mr Grail isn't a person in the *Herald*'s reckoning but a property. And like all property nowadays, he's grossly overvalued. They're not going to risk having his frontage defaced. They'll agree to terms, all right.'

'Outright cancellation of the story?' Becket poured her some beer.

'That, yes. They've dodged stickier ones than this before without blushing. Yes, cancellation. And . . .' – she paused – 'fifteen thousand.'

The others looked at each other, then at the girl. Lanching was frowning. 'Money, you mean?'

She laughed lightly. 'What else do you suggest – cowrie shells?'

'But we agreed to keep money out of it. Christ, Clive won't play along with this, girl. I'm not sure that I should want to, either.'

'My dear Ken, Clive is in no position to have any say in the matter – or he won't be, by tonight. And who's going to believe that he's in real life-and-death danger for the sake of small-town ethics, for God's sake?'

'It's quite true,' Becket put in mildly, 'that our employers tend to be money-orientated, if that's the phrase. You could have a point, Birdie.'

Lanching's lips had been moving. 'Three and three-quarter thou apiece would at least be *some* compensation for what we've put up with in this bloody place.'

'Pay my fine tomorrow,' remarked Becket.

'Christ, I'd forgotten about that. Hey – we'll be unable to produce our star witness.' Lanching grinned happily into his beer.

'Five,' Birdie said. 'Actually.'

They stared at her.

'What do you mean, five?'

'Five thousand. Not three and three quarters.'

Her meaning dawned first on Lanching. 'Oh, come on – you can't cut the poor bugger out. He's going to be the one to be hammered if anything goes wrong.'

'I don't think you understand, Ken. We're not "cutting him out" in any mean-minded sense of dividing loot. We are showing respect for his conscience, as he defined it last night. And for his public image, of course. That above all.'

Becket regarded her levelly.

'You're a hard bitch,' he said. He made it sound like a compliment.

'I think,' said Birdie after a while, 'that there ought to be a note at some stage. Something more tangible than a phone call.'

Lanching looked doubtful. 'It would increase risk,' he said.

'We do need to bear in mind,' Becket said, 'that at worst the police could be called in. If they are, we don't want them crawling round after samples of handwriting and taking our fingerprints.'

'Not yours, anyway,' Birdie said. 'You'll be a convicted felon by then. Careless driving, no less.'

Becket raised a finger. 'Which reminds me. What is old Heckington going to think about the kidnapping of the world's favourite columnist?'

'He isn't going to hear about it unless we tell him.'

'We can scarcely avoid it,' Lanching said.

'OK. Well, he's not going to spend one minute longer than necessary in this place once he gets out of court. He'll be on the first London train after Bob's case.'

Upstairs, Grail was slumped despondently across a small bed. His white hair had been tangled and left bunched over one eye by his concealment under the rug. He picked at his teeth with the nail of his little finger, which he sucked from time to time as if it had been collecting nourishment.

Beside the bed was a card table and a chair. There was a two-bar electric fire near the window, the view from which was restricted by the foliage of a large walnut tree about ten yards distant. Apart from the table, chair and fire, and a much worn rug by the bed, the room was unfurnished. It was also bare of decoration. There was a packing case in one corner, and several cardboard boxes had been stacked along one wall. Against another stood the projection equipment from London and the three film containers.

While Grail was gloomily surveying these unpromising surroundings, his gaze was held by the film cans. For several seconds, he glowered at them with an expression of malevolence that might have surprised his readers. Then he sprang to his feet, wrenched open the door and shouted: 'Are we never going to get any bleeding food today?'

Chapter Eleven

MRS PATMORE RETURNED ON THE QUARTER-PAST FOUR BUS and announced that she was very sorry to be unable to oblige any longer, but her sister in Flax was far from well and blood was thicker than water, whatever Mr Stamper might say, and she therefore would be on the six o'clock back to town and did they want anything cooking first?

Birdie avoided looking relieved. No, she said, there was no need for Mrs Patmore to trouble herself with anything beyond her family obligations. She and her colleagues had arranged to have a meal out that evening. This they would do just as soon as Mr Grail came back from his walk. She, Mrs Patmore, had not happened to see any sign of Mr Grail, had she, since his departure during the morning?

The housekeeper shook her head. 'He reckoned he might go out Gosby and Moldham way,' she said. 'He's been a fairish old while, hasn't he?'

'That's what we were thinking,' Birdie replied. She tried to sound concerned, but not worried enough to shake Mrs Patmore's resolution to abandon her post.

'Never mind, he'll turn up: he looks a gentleman well able to look after himself.' Mrs Patmore took a step towards the stairs.

'Oh, by the way . . .'

'Yes, love?'

'Just a point I thought I ought to mention, Mrs Patmore. That little bedroom at the back . . .'

'I know, yes.'

'It's locked. Mr Grail locked it. There's some quite valuable camera equipment in there, and it did seem sensible to take no risks with it.'

'You know best about things like that,' observed Mrs Patmore, without overtones, and resumed her journey upstairs.

'Pray God,' said Birdie to Becket and Lanching when she re-entered the sitting-room, 'that he keeps quiet long enough for her to get clear. What was he doing when you went up just now?'

Lanching replied. 'Nothing, actually. I think he was nearly asleep. Of course, those drinks before lunch will have made him a bit dopey.'

'It wouldn't be a bad idea if . . .' Birdie stopped, listened. 'Oh, no!' She went to the window. A car was drawing up on the gravel.

'Who is it?' Becket was on his feet.

Birdie gestured him to keep out of sight. 'Tall bloke. Fair hair.

Middle-aged. Never seen him before. Rather a clapped-out car.'

The bell rang.

'I'll get rid of him.' Becket was out of the room before Birdie could object. She stared after him. A voice in the hall, friendly, inquiring, exchanging greetings with the departing Mrs Patmore. The front door closed gently. Footsteps approached.

Becket made the introduction.

'Detective Inspector Purbright, from Flaxborough. He would like to talk to Clive.'

Purbright dispensed a smile to Birdie, to Lanching a nod of acknowledgment. He sat in the chair indicated by the girl.

'Mr Becket,' he said, 'has told me that Mr Grail is not in.'

'No,' Birdie said, 'we seem . . .' (the very slight pause bespoke rapid calculation of the odds for and against Purbright's being the sort of policeman who might appreciate a lightness of attitude) 'to have mislaid him.'

Purbright gave her another smile. 'Mr Grail doesn't happen to have gone to be measured for pistols, does he?'

'Nothing so dramatic,' Birdie said. 'So far as we know, he's simply enjoying the novelty of a country walk. However' – she shrugged, as if sympathizing with the policeman – 'we do get your drift.'

'Is Mr Grail likely to be long?'

'He should be here now, really,' Becket said. Birdie gave him a quick glance of reproof.

'Would you mind my waiting for ten minutes or so?' Purbright asked. 'The matter isn't all that urgent – or I hope not, anyway – and one doesn't like to make double journeys if they can be avoided.'

'Perhaps we can help.' The suggestion came from Lanching.

'Possibly, sir. At least you will know from all the fuss in the newspapers that your Mr Grail has attracted the attention of one of our more colourful citizens.'

'With a little help, we suspect.'

'How do you mean, sir?'

Becket spoke. 'We think your loony mayor was put up to it. By a little plump fellow, for one. Optician, or something.'

'Ah, Mr Barrington Hoole. He comes from Chalmsbury, the next town.'

'Also,' said Birdie, 'your local editor, inspector. The one with the Cheshire cat grin.'

'He has, hasn't he,' Purbright acknowledged fondly, then looked more serious. 'But apart from questions of eccentric behaviour and possible breaches of the law by excited gentlemen waving pistols about, you will appreciate that the police must take notice of what Mr Grail apparently intends to allege concerning pornographic films.'

'Nothing's been printed yet,' Becket said, grumpily.

'Oh, come, Mr Becket. Even a person as unsubtle as myself could be in no doubt after reading Sunday's piece that the purpose of forthcoming articles is to describe these films and to identify local people responsible for making them. Am I wrong?'

'That is really a question for Grail, inspector,' said Lanching. 'We are a team, in a sense, but ultimately he's the one who's responsible for the column.'

Purbright inclined his head, as if satisfied. He turned to Birdie.

'Miss Clemenceaux, I understand from my chief constable that your role in this team is that of researcher. You gather preliminary information, is that so?'

'More or less, yes.'

'That must be a very interesting part of the work. Tell me, in the course of whatever research you did on this particular story, did you hear mention of a rather sad accident that happened here in Flaxborough about a year ago – one associated with film-making, I mean?' Suddenly, the inspector leaned forward and smiled apologetically. 'Oh, I don't mean pornographic film-making, of course. And I am not asking you to betray confidences. I am just mildly curious, that's all.'

'I do recall,' said Birdie, 'something in the national papers. "Death in the Darkroom" – that sort of thing. A young woman. But no one I've spoken to up here has mentioned it.'

'Indeed? Well, I suppose they had no occasion to. She was a keen member of this local society, though. And her husband, too. A singularly tragic little family – if family's the word. They had no children.'

After a pause, Lanching asked: 'The husband – he still lives here in the town, does he? Although' – he glanced at Birdie – 'I'm sure I'm not trespassing on Grail's territory if I tell you that neither of them is mentioned in the story as it stands.'

'Just as well, sir,' said Purbright, 'if only for the sake of whatever relatives there may be. Actually, he was from another part of the country altogether.'

'And he's returned there?' prompted Birdie.

Purbright looked pained, as if something he had said was being misconstrued. 'Oh, but he's dead, Miss Clemenceaux. Curiously enough, I heard about it only this morning. He died four or five weeks ago. In London, I understand.'

Becket was frowning deeply. 'If he died a month ago, how was it you took so long to find out?'

'But I wasn't trying to find out, Mr Becket, was I?'

Becket shrugged and looked away.

'In that case, inspector,' said Birdie, 'I certainly find it curious, to use your word, that this man's death happened to come to your notice this morning.'

'The inquiries into Henry Bush's background were being made by people quite unconnected with the police,' said Purbright. 'I'm just one of those unfortunates who always get the telephone calls that no one else wants to answer.'

'Are you going to tell us who the interested party was?' Birdie asked.

Purbright smiled, but said nothing.

Soon afterwards, he rose.

'It seems that Mr Grail's engagement is keeping him a rather long time. Perhaps he'll be good enough to give me a ring when he comes back. I shall be at the police station until at least six.'

'He only went for a walk,' Birdie said, with a hint of defensiveness in her voice.

'Perhaps,' suggested the inspector, 'he was tempted further afield than he meant to go. It's a very attractive time of year in the country.'

As soon as Purbright's car had passed from sight of the house, Birdie hurried upstairs.

'Christikins! We've got a right rozzer to contend with there, old son. Listen, just what do you know – and have kept to yourself, I don't have to add – about that Bush woman and her husband?'

Grail was sitting hunched between the bed and the electric fire, both bars of which he had switched on. He spoke with his eyes half closed, as though in pain.

'For God's sake, don't be incoherent. Another hour of being walled up like a nun and I shall lose my reason.'

She sat on the bed, gave the now almost empty gin bottle a frown of disgust, and said slowly: 'That man who has just left is a police inspector. He pretends he is interested in preventing mayhem by duelling pistol. In fact – and I'm bloody sure I'm not imagining this – he is most horribly curious about that girl who died of poisoning in a darkroom and about what happened to the widower. This, dear Clivikins, is a complication we could well have done without. Kindly conquer your alcoholic self-pity and lend it some thought.'

Grail released his hold on his knees and moved away from the fire.

'Look,' he said, wearily, 'I can't tell you any more than you know now. I can't tell you who these Bush people are or were, except that they did belong to this photographic society thing. Nor can I tell you who originally tipped us the story. If I knew, I'd be out there committing murder. Lastly, I cannot tell you how anyone came to appoint as news correspondent a man so moronic as to accept that film at its face value. Now leave me to stay kidnapped in peace until this whole dreadful business is over.'

The girl surveyed him for some moments. 'I should have thought,' she said at last, 'that some small expression of gratitude wouldn't pain you too deeply. Bob and Ken and I are the ones who have the dirty work to do.'

'Concocting a spurious phone call doesn't sound too onerous a task. It should appeal to that sense of humour of yours, Birdie. "Oh, Mr Richardson, and they say they'll send you one of poor Clive's ears if you don't agree to their demands." '

'Don't tempt me, mate. Don't bloody tempt me.'

Grail turned to see her face unexpectedly pale and tight-featured. He spread his hands in token of contrition. 'You're very sweet, actually. And I do realize what the team's taken on for me. Great.' He tried to slip a conciliatory hand beneath her skirt.

'Oh, for Christ's sake, Clive.' Stepping quickly to the door, she opened it. 'Don't push your luck. Stay put. We'll bring you something up when we get a meal organized.'

Purbright found the coroner's officer anxious to talk to him when he arrived back in Fen Street.

'That insurance company has been on the phone again,' Sergeant Malley announced. 'Their fire assessor is not very happy about Bush's accident.'

'We knew that already, Bill. I don't see how we can help, though.'

'For one thing, they asked if they could have a transcript of the inquest on his wife.'

The inspector pursed his lips. 'I suppose so. For what it's worth. What are they looking for – coincidences?'

Malley compressed a couple of chins against his tunic collar as he peered down into the bowl of the short, black pipe that he was excavating. Breathing seemed a fairly hard job for him.

'Aye, well, one is fairly obvious. They both were mucking about with cine film at the time.'

'Nobody's suggested that the husband – Henry, was it? – was poisoned, though, surely?'

'Good lord, no. He was incinerated. Plus most of his flat, apparently. It went up in minutes.'

'I presume,' said Purbright, 'that the object of the insurance company's solicitude is to avoid paying out some money. So what does it hope to prove – that Henry committed suicide out of grief for his late wife?'

Malley shook his head and puffed his cheeks in refutation. 'Mr Bush, as I understand it, wasn't much given to grief. He was a bit of a one for the totties, they tell me. Both before and after his missus passed on.'

'Very well, then, Bill. What *do* the insurance people want to believe? That he was done in?'

The sergeant squinted down his pipe stem. 'I reckon they'd settle for that. Aye.'

'I fail to see what we can do to help at this end. The fellow's wife certainly couldn't be proved to have been murdered. There was no one near her at the time. Indications of accident were straightforward enough. And there wasn't a whisper of anybody wishing to harm her – for insurance or any other reason.'

Malley grunted. He gave the inspector a glance that was partly speculative, partly sceptical. 'So we kept saying at the time,' he said.

Purbright was examining his sleeve. 'What else did your London friends tell you, Bill?'

'Not much. There was something queer about the fire, though. Very violent, he said. Almost explosive. And they found traces afterwards of celluloid.'

'Which would explain the violence.'

'Aye. But modern film isn't made of celluloid. Not any kind that Bush might have been using, anyway. They think he must have had several reels of really old-fashioned stuff lying about in there.'

'Open?'

'Unwound, even. That's the theory. I said nowt. You get on with it, mate, I thought. I wasn't going to have him quoting a copper from two hundred miles away to help them upset a verdict that their own coroner's already recorded.'

'The inquest wasn't adjourned, then?' Purbright asked.

'Oh, no. Death by misadventure. That was that, apparently.'

'In that case,' said the inspector, 'let us continue to plough our own furrow, Bill.' After a pause, he added: 'Still, it's interesting to know what's been turned up in another corner of the field, isn't it?'

Malley continued for a while to scoop tarry fragments from his pipe bowl. Purbright recognized in the sergeant's lingering a sign that he would, in the fullness of time, either impart a piece of surprising information or make a suggestion that he feared might be unwelcome. He waited.

The quantity of pipe reamings that Malley caught in his big, cupped hand eventually satisfied him as adequate and he tipped them carefully into an old envelope, which he folded, re-folded, and dropped into the inspector's waste-paper basket. Purbright caught a whiff of what a whaler's forecastle must have been like after a five-year voyage.

'Old-fashioned,' said Malley, reflectively. He pocketed the pipe, snorted a little breath in and out of his nose, and added: 'I've been thinking about that.'

'Oh, yes?'

'Well, there was that film that cremated poor old Henry – if we're to take the word of whoever investigated the fire . . .'

'The police, presumably,' interposed Purbright.

'Aye, London police,' the sergeant amended carefully. He went on: 'Well, that film was old-fashioned, out of date, not the sort that's used any more. Bloody dangerous, and all. Right?'

'Certainly, if it was celluloid.'

The fat man gave two more of his little clearance snorts. 'Now go back to the wife's death. That stuff she swallowed in her coffee was a film-processing chemical. One of the cyanide salts. Sodium, was it? I can't remember which, but it doesn't matter. The point is, it was a chemical that's not used any more. Bloody dangerous. Out of date. Old-fashioned.'

Purbright gave the matter thought. 'Pretty tenuous,' he said, at last.

The sergeant looked encouraged. He nodded. 'Just what *I* thought.'

'Ah,' said Purbright.

Chapter Twelve

THE MANAGING EDITOR OF THE *Sunday Herald* WAS, AT HALF past four that afternoon, suddenly and urgently desirous of conversation with Clive Grail. His personal assistant, a young man who could speak English and look up telephone numbers, made the call. Becket answered.

'It's Richardson,' Becket said to Birdie, his hand over the mouthpiece.

'Christ, he's quick off the mark. Never mind, here we go.' And she took the phone. 'I could say that I was just about to ring you, Mr Richardson, but that would not be true. I had intended to telephone at six o'clock if the situation had not changed. The fact is that we are having the teeniest bit of worry up here.'

'Grail. I asked for Grail. Didn't they tell you I asked for Grail? You're Miss, er . . . Yes, I didn't ask – how do you mean worry? Put Grail on, will you, miss, er . . .'

'He is not here, Mr Richardson. This is Birdie Clemenceaux.

Mr Grail went out some hours ago. And that is why we are a little anxious.'

'Out? Where's out? There's nothing there to go out to, is there? My info was that it's some kind of a village.'

'Flaxborough is a market town of several thousand inhabitants, in point of fact, but what I . . .'

'In point of nothing, Miss Clemenceaux. What are you trying to tell me? I simply want to talk to Grail. Go shout for him. Loud. Won't do you any harm. I was raised on a farm in New South Wales. You don't know what distances are.'

Birdie said very patiently: 'Mr Grail left the house about six hours ago. He said he would take a walk to clear a headache. He did not return for lunch. He has not been in touch by telephone. There probably is a perfectly simple explanation, and I should not have bothered you yet if you had not happened to ring. But the story Mr Grail has been preparing is, as you know, a delicate one; and local feelings have run a little high.'

She waited, knowing that some of the things she had said would be filtering by now into the managing editor's consciousness.

Several seconds passed.

'Very worrying,' said Richardson, with newfound gravity.

'Oh, I wouldn't go so far as . . .'

'Extremely worrying,' he said. 'Do you have,' Richardson asked after a further interval for thought, 'some sort of a village constable around the place?'

Birdie resisted the temptation to say yes, but he's mending the stocks at the moment. She suggested instead that no police force would take kindly to being asked to mount a search in broad daylight for an able-bodied adult who had missed his lunch.

'Right, we'll give him another couple of hours,' said Richardson, grudgingly. 'But keep in touch. I'll be here until eight or nine. After that, you can reach me at home.' He handed the phone to his personal assistant, who told her the number of what he defined carefully as 'Mr Richardson's private residence in Addington Park.' (It felt like getting the MBE, Birdie told Lanching afterwards.)

Grail had heard the ringing of the telephone. He appeared at the head of the staircase. 'Was that for me?'

Birdie hastened aloft. She pushed him back into his room. 'If you don't want me to lock that bloody door, you'd better stop acting like a kid sick of a party. And I mean that, brotherkins, so you can bloody well get used to the idea.'

Grail stared at her, his mouth slightly open and moving as if trying to shape elusive words. Confinement already was rendering him slightly shabby-looking. The long, aesthetic face had slipped from its cast of philosophic calm and in that moment gave the impression merely of stupidity.

'And what the hell have *I* done?' he complained.

Birdie ignored the question. 'That was Richardson,' she said, 'so everything will have to go off that little bit earlier than we'd planned. Not that it matters. Your kidnappers are very accommodating gentlemen. They wait for us to tell them when to ring.'

'When are you going to get on to the office again?'

'About seven.'

'We decided it should be a lot later than that.' Grail had sat down and tidied his hair – with a comb, not the nursery brush in his inner pocket – and was making an effort to recover some of his authoritative poise.

Birdie shook her head. 'Richardson's even more jumpy than I expected him to be. If we don't produce a good juicy threat by fairly early evening, he'll insist on the police being called in, and that'll knacker the whole auction.'

Grail regarded her for some moments, then said: 'I hope you really are as confident as you were pretending yesterday. Has something gone wrong that you're trying to keep to yourself?'

'Nothing's gone wrong. Why should you think that?'

'Because,' said Grail, 'experience has taught me to mistrust these sudden plunges of yours into a bar-room vernacular. They usually mean that you're up to something.'

'Clive!' She leaned down, gently implanted a kiss in his left ear, and stepped to the door. 'You aren't used to these criminal enterprises, that's all. You're bound to become a bit touchy.' She grinned, added: 'I forgive you, though,' and was gone.

Birdie rang the *Herald* a few minutes after seven o'clock. When she was put through to Richardson, she announced at once that something very serious had happened and suggested that the proprietor, Mr Oscar Murphy, be brought into consultation without delay.

Richardson put the proposal to his personal assistant, who pointed out in the most matter-of-fact manner that Mr Murphy was in Tahiti. Perhaps the conversation could be taped for transmission? Perhaps it could, said Richardson. The personal assistant turned a switch and pressed a button.

'Very well, Miss Clemenceaux. Spill.'

She began to speak. There was a slight tremble in her voice and she paused after every sentence to take breath. Twice during the recital, Richardson urged her not to be frightened. She took this to be a cue for making a brave swallowing sound while she checked her notes before resuming.

There had been a phone call, she said, a little before seven. It sounded like a local line, quite clear and without connection delays. The voice was that of a man. Nothing very special about it in the way of accent or style of speech. Local, she thought, but not uneducated. Sort of middle class. But very cold, very hostile. A little bit mad, one might almost say.

'The first thing he said was: "My friends and I are entertaining somebody you know. If you want to know him again, you'd better do exactly as I'm about to tell you. You will get in touch at once with this somebody's employers and inform them that unless they promise in writing not to publish somebody's pack of lies about our town we propose to take him off their payroll for life."

'I tried to interrupt at that point and find if the call was a spoof of some kind. For one thing, Grail's name hadn't been mentioned. And the language was so melodramatic. One reads about these kidnap messages, but when you hear one actually coming over the phone, it just isn't believable.

'Anyway, whoever it was didn't give me a chance to argue. He ploughed straight on. I quote. "You will tell the *Sunday Herald* to put a piece in the paper on Sunday next saying that because of circumstances etcetera – you know how these things are put – the article that was to have appeared will not now be printed, and the *Sunday Herald* offers apologies to those who have been caused distress." '

'Apologies!' The managing editor might as well have been

requested to blow up his own presses.

'That is not all,' Birdie added, 'I'm afraid.'

Richardson, still in shock, made no comment.

'Money was stipulated,' she said. 'Quite a lot. They – whoever they are – demand fifteen thousand pounds. Only they expressed it rather unpleasantly.'

'How do you mean, unpleasantly?' It was clear that in Mr Richardson's view, disbursement of newspaper funds could be nothing other than unpleasant.

' "Fifteen hundred a finger" was how the man on the phone put it,' Birdie explained quietly. 'He said that if it wasn't paid, they would see that Clive never typed another story.' She made a pause suggestive of shuddering. 'A finger for every day's delay, he said.'

'Good God!' said Richardson.

'There was one other thing.' Birdie put this in quickly; she had nearly forgotten a very important safeguard.

'Yes?'

'There must be no approach made to the police. If that happens, Clive will be killed at once.'

'The usual empty threat, Miss Clemenceaux.'

Oh, hell . . . No, perhaps the man-of-the-world act was strictly for Murphy's consumption on tape. She lowered her voice almost to a whisper. 'No, Mr Richardson. Not this time.'

A pause. 'You think not?'

Ah, that was better. The old Dither-Dick. She said: 'I'm certain. Don't ask me why. I just am.'

Another pause. 'Did this . . . this kidnapper or whatever he is . . . did he say anything about how the money should be paid? If we do pay, that is, and you realize it cannot be my decision.'

'He said further instructions would be given tonight.'

'By phone?'

'I assume so. Because' (a splendid idea had just flashed into her mind) 'he also said something about arranging for us to hear Clive's voice. "While he still has one," he said. I really think he must be quite horribly dangerous, this man. You must believe me, Mr Richardson.'

'I do, Birdie; I do, indeed.'

First name sympathy. Excellent. 'I think I ought to clear the line now, in case they come on again. And please, please don't let anyone tell the police. Not yet. This isn't London. Every policeman here is known, in or out of uniform. And whoever's got poor Clive will be on the watch.'

No man who owns five newspaper chains, sundry television stations and magazines in half the countries of the world dares remain for more than a very short time out of touch with one or another of his deputy money-makers, so it was a matter for no great surprise when the managing editor of the London *Sunday Herald* was summoned in the middle of his evening meal to take a telephone call from Tahiti.

Mr Oscar Murphy wanted to be assured, before he went back down the beach for a clam 'n' yam bake, that somebody had remembered to raise by two per cent the classified advertisement rate in the north-eastern and Scottish circulation areas.

Richardson said yes, this had been done, and, hold on, sir, there had arisen a problem of great urgency, on which the immediate ruling of Mr Murphy would be much appreciated. The paper's star columnist had been kidnapped. Clive Grail.

'What for? Money?'

'Yes, sir. Partly, anyway.'

'How much?'

'Fifteen thousand pounds.'

'What do we pay Grail?'

'Twelve, sir, I believe.'

'Wrong – it's twelve and a half.' A brief pause. Richardson fancied he could hear Pacific surf, but it doubtless was something to do with transmission. 'OK. Pay up.'

'There is another condition, Mr Murphy. For Grail's life being spared, I mean.'

'Namely?'

'We cancel a piece of his that was to have been published in the next issue.'

'Set already, I suppose?'

'Substantially, sir.'

'Costed yet?'

Oh, God. 'I could get a figure first thing in the morning.'

'Any secondary rights sold?'

'None,' declared Richardson, confident of approval.

'Should be. This crap's a commodity, not a sacred relic.'

There was a further short interval. Then Mr Murphy signified that the kidnappers' terms should be met, provided that there were reasonable grounds to suppose their threat serious. He stipulated, however, that somebody would have to make a detailed report to him at the end of the week of what arrangements had been made within the editorial account to recover the costs of the affair.

Richardson ate no more dinner. He returned at once to his office and rang Flaxborough.

Lanching answered. No, he was sorry, but Miss Clemenceaux had just left to fetch food from a restaurant in the town. Could he take a méssage?

'She can eat at a time like this?'

Lanching told him that the housekeeper had been called away.

'That's damned suspicious. Don't you think that's damned suspicious?'

It would bear thinking about, Lanching admitted.

'Tell Miss Clemenceaux that Mr Murphy has personally given the all clear ransom-wise. I'll see what can be done tonight on actual cash-raising. Grail's damned lucky he works for a boss with heart. Don't *you* think he's lucky?'

'Most fortunate, Mr Richardson, as are we all. I think we should leave this line free now, though, or it may be suspected that we are in touch with the police.'

From the Yellow River Chinese Take-away in Spoongate, Birdie bore a large carrier bag containing Special Recommended Dinner 'E' and made the return journey to Miriam Lodge swiftly but carefully.

'Warm some plates under the hot tap,' she instructed Becket. She began to unlid the containers, sniffing rapturously. A nest of crispy noodles was revealed. 'Blissikins!' murmured Birdie. To Lanching she said: 'Go up to the Prisoner of Zenda, will you, Ken, and ask him if he wants both King Prawn Balls *and* Sweet-sour Lobster Fries; there aren't all that many of either, and I . . . No, hang on a minute . . .' She stared at the containers, as if wrestling with a conscience. Then she shook her head, decisively. 'No, to hell with it. What he doesn't know about, he won't miss. He can have extra chicken and almonds instead. Lucky lad.' She held out her hands for the plates which Becket had been drying clumsily.

After the meal, Birdie found Grail in a more relaxed mood than she had expected. He had eaten all his food. She eyed the plate. 'Good,' she said, sounding rather like a nurse. She picked up the tray. 'Give me five minutes to get a tape recorder fixed up, and there'll be a little treat for you.'

He regarded her quizzically.

'You're coming for an airing,' she said. 'To a telephone box a couple of hundred yards down the road. It's set back in some shrubbery and I noticed just now that the light isn't working.'

'Ten to one the telephone isn't, either,' said Grail.

But it was.

Becket answered, after Birdie had dialled by touch in the dark.

'For God's sake,' Birdie admonished him, 'don't put any of this through the recorder before Clive starts talking. We might have to play the tape back to London before there's a chance to vet it. So no balls-ups, as you value your sweet life. If you've any doubts, say so.'

Becket said no, everything was fine.

Birdie told him: 'When I say "now", start the tape. Clive will begin about five seconds after that. OK?'

'Sure.'

'Right . . . *Now.*'

She handed the phone to Grail. He seemed to have difficulty in locating it. She caught his hand and guided it.

Grail spoke into the phone. Slowly, hesitantly, he delivered words as if he had been without sleep for days. In the darkness, Birdie nodded approval.

'This . . . this is Clive here. Clive Grail . . . I don't know where I . . . where I am, but you're not to . . . not to try and find me. I'm . . . serious about that. These people . . . These people do mean . . . what they say . . .'

Great, Birdie breathed to herself. She reached and gently patted Grail's arm encouragingly.

After quite a long pause, Grail took two or three deep breaths and went on: 'Nothing has happened . . . to me . . . up to . . . nothing has . . . Oh, God, I'm . . .'

His voice was being made to sound weaker. A plaintive note

had crept in. *Don't ham it, boykins, for Christ's sake,* Birdie urged silently.

'Nothing's . . . oh, God, I . . . oh, God, I . . .'

Speech now was petering out altogether. Birdie felt Grail's knees pressing harder and harder against her within the narrow confines of the kiosk.

'Please, I . . . oh, God . . . please . . .'

She heard the phone clatter down against the glass panels. 'Clive! What is it?' She clutched his arm and tried to hold him upright, but he continued his slow, frightening collapse until he lay jammed diagonally across the floor of the box.

For what seemed to the girl a very long time, there came from the dark bundle at her feet a sound like the spasmodic tearing of canvas.

At last it stopped.

Birdie dragged one leg free and used it to help her lever open the door. The cool night air cleared her head a little but did nothing to diminish her sense of horror and dismay. She pulled herself out of the kiosk allowing the door to swing shut, and stood leaning back against it for some moments. Several cars went by, but shrubs shielded her from the beams of their headlamps.

She opened the door once more, and held it open with her body while she knelt and put her face close to Grail's. She heard no sign of breathing. Not knowing where to test for a pulse, she felt gently around the neck and under the shirt in what she supposed to be the region of the heart. She encountered not the slightest tremor.

There was a noise somewhere, though. An elfin squawking. Close at hand. Birdie looked up, her fear mounting again. Then she realized what the noise was. She reached and grasped the hanging phone.

'What the hell's going on? Are you still supposed to want this recording?' Becket's voice.

She spoke quietly, urgently. 'Bob, now listen. Something absolutely bloody's happened. Clive's had a heart attack or something. He's on the floor here, out cold. Bob . . . Bob, I think he's dead.' She paused, but Becket made no attempt to say anything. She went on: 'Look, one of you will have to get out here quickly. Run, walk, but quickly. It's not far. I daren't leave him. And someone will have to stay by the phone at the house in case the office comes back on. Whoever does come, for Christ's sake be quick.'

She hung up, let the door close, and began her wait outside, an anxious sentry in the dark.

Chapter Thirteen

IT WAS LANCHING WHO CAME. BIRDIE COULD HEAR HIS footsteps, at a half run, and his laboured breathing before she discerned the figure, close to the side of the road.

'Ken?'

He stopped, looked about him, then hurried to the car.

Birdie took his arm. 'He's on the floor. In the telephone box.'

Lanching pulled open the door and knelt. His shoulders were still heaving with the effort of running. After a few seconds, he leaned low and listened closely, head on one side. He unfastened buttons and felt around. Again he listened.

'He's dead all right. No doubt about that.'

She stared at Lanching's upturned face, a white blur in the darkness. 'But you can't be sure. Not without proper tests.'

'What are we going to do?'

'We shall have to get him to hospital, that's all.' The girl spoke firmly, but she made no move. When Lanching remained silent, she added: 'We must, Ken. Christ, it's the least that anybody could do.' But still she stood, irresolute.

'I agree.' Lanching opened the rear door of the car. 'Look, if I pull him in from inside, will you help with the weight?'

It took them nearly ten minutes of rolling, pulling, dragging and hoisting to transfer Grail's body from kiosk to car. When the door was shut at last, Birdie leaned back against the car and passed trembling fingers across her brow. Her pallor seemed in the dark to have taken on a greenish tinge.

'It's so bloody undignified,' she said.

'Yes.'

'For him, I mean.'

'Yes, I knew what you meant.'

She walked to the driver's side. 'At least the poor bastard won't be worrying about snake bites this time.'

'Snake bites?'

'In that derelict station. He said there were snakes. Touch of the neurotikins, I should imagine.'

Lanching took his seat beside Birdie and watched her start the engine and steer the car in an arc until it faced the direction from which they had come.

'We aren't taking him to hospital, then, I gather,' he said, quietly.

Her reply was little more than a whisper. 'There doesn't seem much point.'

He waited, then said: 'He *is* dead, you know. I'm quite sure. This resuscitation business is only playing with reflexes. It's cruel.'

It was almost midnight when the Rolls returned. Becket was standing framed against the open front door of the house. At once he went back inside. The others followed him to the sitting-room. Already he was asking where the hell they had been.

Silently, the girl poured drinks. She motioned the others to sit, then took a chair herself. She swallowed some of her brandy.

'There is no point,' she said at last, 'in pretending that we are not, to some extent, in the shit. But this is the time for sensible appraisals, not for blowing of tops.' She gazed calmly at Becket. 'You want to know where the hell we've been and I'll tell you. Hell's not a bad description, actually. We've carried poor old corpsikins Clive to that derelict railway station where he was hiding earlier. And we've dumped him. In the ticket office, actually. OK?'

Becket stared at her for several seconds, then turned away. 'Christ . . .'

'As you say. Christ. But what *should* we have done, do you think? Assuming that you *have* been thinking.'

'Listen, girl, you'd have been thinking all right if you'd had a phone call all to yourself from that Aussie hard hat Richardson.'

Birdie and Lanching exchanged glances. 'When was that?' Lanching asked Becket.

'About an hour ago. Fortunately, he didn't take it into his

head to ask if you were here, Ken. He third-degreed me about Birdie, though, as if it was her who'd been bloody kidnapped. The man just goes on and on. You can't get anything across to him.'

'What did you say?' Birdie asked.

Becket shrugged impatiently. 'Something about your having been called away. I don't know – I left it pretty vague on purpose. In the end I got rid of him with your dodge about keeping the line open for kidnappers. And I might add that I felt a bloody charlie.'

'I'm afraid,' said Birdie, 'that from now on none of us is going to be able to indulge in the luxury of embarrassment in face of melodrama. Unless, of course' – she paused to look steadily at each of the two men in turn – 'unless you feel that the only way out of this mess is to tell the truth about it.'

'To the paper, you mean?' asked Lanching.

'To the paper, obviously. But also to the police. Poor Clive clinched that as soon as he had his heart attack, or whatever.' She smiled. 'God, I shouldn't put it past him to have kicked off deliberately. Awkward old sod.' The smile faded. She stared bleakly at her hands.

'The money was a bad idea.' Lanching's voice was gentle, matter-of-fact.

'Oh, by the way . . .' Becket began.

Birdie interrupted, looking at Lanching. 'How do you mean, bad?'

'Well, it commits us, doesn't it?'

The girl nodded. 'I think it does. The ironic thing about it is that an invention we added to the story for the sake of realism has now made it too damned real.' She clenched her hand. 'Christ, of all the moments to pick to . . .'

Lanching completed the tailed-off sentence. '. . . to die?'

'I can just imagine,' Birdie said, 'a policeman's face when we explain that because a blue film scandal proved not to be scandalous after all we first fixed up a phony kidnapping and then made it look real by extorting fifteen thousand quid out of our employers, at which moment the supposed kidnappee happened to drop dead.'

Becket seized his chance. 'I was trying to tell you . . .'

She glanced at him. 'Sorry, Bob.'

'Heckington's coming over. Probably by a night train. He's bringing the money. Used notes. They thought that would be what was wanted.'

'Heckington?' echoed Lanching.

'The barrister,' Birdie reminded him. 'Sir Arthur. I suppose Richardson imagines you've only to produce a British QC and criminals will say sorry and pack it in.'

'One thing's sure,' Becket said. 'He'll be for telling the police right away. He'll do it himself if we won't.'

Birdie shook her head. 'Sir Arthur will do precisely what he has always done – what he gets paid for. He will obey the instructions of Herald Newspapers Limited.' She paused. 'Incidentally, does either of you know if Clive was being treated for heart trouble or anything? Did he ever say?'

'There were those white things he was always taking,' said Lanching. 'Those capsules.'

'After meals, that was,' Becket added.

'Probably just antacid capsules, then,' said Birdie. 'I remember he used to stuff them down fairly liberally. No, it's just that I'd feel happier if I were sure that the police would have no possible grounds for thinking that we . . . you know, had sort of helped the poor sod's exit.'

Both men stared at her.

'Why on earth should they think that?' Lanching asked.

'I should have thought it fairly obvious. They are not likely to be predisposed in our favour when they hear that the kidnapping was a fraud.'

'But it was Clive's idea,' Becket said.

'And how do we prove that?' Birdie went back to the sideboard and replenished her drink. With a gesture she invited the others to offer their glasses. 'The money part wasn't his idea,' she said.

'We haven't had any money yet,' said Becket. 'We can tell Heckington to take it back.'

It was Lanching's turn to make objection. 'No. That would just be interpreted as panic. It wouldn't alter the way things are going to seem to the police. I think Birdie's right. Confessions are out.'

The telephone began ringing.

They looked at one another, startled as if by a development totally unexpected.

Lanching broke the tension. 'Must be the kidnappers.'

Becket laughed.

Birdie put a finger to her lips, waited a few moments, then lifted the receiver.

It was Richardson. He sounded annoyed and bewildered. 'I do think, Miss Clemenceaux, that you might do more to keep us informed at this end. It's extremely . . .'

She interrupted him firmly. He talked on against her for some moments, but finally stalled and asked her with some show of concern to repeat something she had just said.

'I told you I had made contact with these people. Personal contact.'

There was a pause. 'Go on,' he said.

'I got back only a couple of minutes before you rang. It was a man. I didn't see him, of course. And there was nothing special about his voice. The appointment was made by phone and at such short notice – deliberately, I suppose – that I couldn't have arranged to be followed. In any case, they'd repeated their threat about Mr Grail, so I wouldn't have dared.'

'And where was the appointment? I don't quite understand what you mean about not seeing this man.'

'If you must know, I was told to go to a ladies' lavatory in an all-night car park in town – here in Flaxborough, that is.'

Becket and Lanching exchanged awed glances. Birdie, listening to Richardson with undisguised impatience, winked at them.

'Do you mean to say you met this man – by arrangement – in a ladies' lavatory?' The managing editor sounded deeply shocked.

Birdie resisted the temptation to make a flippant retort. 'He was standing outside apparently,' she said. 'There's a public path there. He spoke through a ventilator in the wall. I could hear him all right, but there was nothing about the voice that I should recognize again.'

'What had he to say concerning the money?'

'Only that it would have to be delivered by me and nobody else.'

'Delivered?'

'That's the word he used.'

'Did he give you an address?'

Birdie directed a glance of despair at the ceiling. 'It was scarcely likely that he would do that, Mr Richardson. I assume that I shall get further instructions over the phone.'

There was a grunt from Richardson. 'Sir Arthur Heckington is bringing the money personally. He is on the night train, I understand. And Miss Clemenceaux . . .'

'Yes?'

'I wish you to leave the handling of this affair to him. He is more used to this sort of thing.'

'What, kidnapping?'

'I think,' said Richardson, crossly, 'that you know what I mean. Negotiations. Handling criminals. The law is his business, after all.'

'Of course.' Birdie suppressed a yawn with difficulty. She was just beginning to realize how tired she was.

'That tape,' she said, after Richardson had rung off. 'We ought to check it now, while we are still on our own.'

The emergence of Grail's voice from the recorder's little speaker had something of the heartless quality of clinical experiment. Grave-faced, all three, they listened to the words growing slower, more distorted by distress and pain.

Birdie shook her head. 'Poor sod – I thought he was hamming it up.'

'I suppose,' said Lanching, hesitantly, 'that we're listening to him actually dying. It's there – on record.'

Becket suddenly gave a start. 'One good thing,' he said. 'That tape does at least put us absolutely in the clear. I mean, if we *had* been to blame for old Clive's death, it's damn hard to believe that he'd have rung us up specially for us to get it on tape.'

They ran the tape through once again.

Birdie looked thoughtful. 'There is one danger,' she said. 'After hearing how Clive sounds on that recording, is Heckington going to suggest demanding further proof of his survival?'

'He wouldn't be that heartless, surely,' said Lanching.

'He's a lawyer,' said Birdie. 'Those boys part with money like it was penisectomy.'

'I can't see that it matters,' Becket said. 'Clive was no great buddy of mine, but I don't fancy making money out of the poor bugger's heart attack.'

'Not five thousand?' Birdie asked quietly.

Becket puffed his cheeks, then shrugged. 'I don't think we've considered the risks properly. God knows what the police will dig up. They're not fools.'

'What is there *for* them to dig up?' Lanching asked.

'God, there's always *something*. They make sure of that.'

Birdie smiled. 'There speaks a man with one foot in gaol. Don't worry, Bob – you'll have enough now to pay your fine.' She rose. 'I'll make coffee.'

At a quarter past one, the telephone rang at the bedside of the managing editor of the *Sunday Herald*. He was not asleep, and told Miss Clemenceaux so in a manner that made her introductory apologies seem an unwarranted reflection upon his sense of duty.

'We have heard from Mr Grail,' she announced. 'The call came through about ten minutes ago. We managed to get most of what he said recorded on a little tape machine of mine. Would you like me to play it back for you now? You'll need to listen carefully; it may not transmit all that well.'

Richardson did listen carefully and with a deepening frown. 'And there was nothing after that?'

'Nothing. They just rang off.'

'To me, Grail sounds in a pretty bad way. Didn't you think he sounded in a pretty bad way?'

Birdie hesitated. 'In a sense, yes. But he would be very upset. Frightened, too, I should think. That would be perfectly natural.'

'I heard the word "God" several times. Quite definitely. Didn't you hear that? I did.'

'At least we know he's alive, Mr Richardson. We must just hope for the best.'

'I never saw much built on hopes, not in the newspaper business. However, you must let Sir Arthur be responsible for decisions. Is that all you recorded, by the way? Grail's message?'

Richardson's woodenly unsympathetic manner was beginning to anger the girl. It also had the curious effect of lending self-conviction to her inventiveness.

'Now look, Mr Richardson, it is easy enough to be critical afterwards, but telephone calls from kidnappers are not day-today events that one takes in one's stride. The *Herald* doesn't pay me or my colleagues to be electronics engineers. I suggest that our having got anything at all on tape does deserve a bit of credit.'

'No good going through life waiting to have your head patted, Miss Clemenceaux. What else did these people have to say?'

'They gave instructions,' she replied, coldly, 'for the payment of the money.'

There was a pause. 'Well?'

'I know what the instructions are. I think that is enough.'

'Miss Clemenceaux – this is not your money.'

Lanching and Becket saw a smile glimmer faintly and die. 'The line,' she said, 'may be tapped, for all I know. I do have a certain responsibility, Mr Richardson. These people are not playing games.'

'Very well. But remember. There's one hell of a disbursement involved. I have to account for it. And you will have your share of accounting to do as well.'

With which dour declaration, the managing editor rang off and lay, unblinking, flat and rigid in his single bed. The light remained burning until morning when his wife entered from the adjoining room, switched it off, and called him 'dear'.

Chapter Fourteen

'DEAR GOD, DON'T TELL ME THAT THEY WENT OFF AND fought their wretched duel in secret. *Where* did you say he was found, Bill? A railway station?'

'It was once. Hambourne. Aye, they found him in what used to be the booking office, I understand.'

'Who did?'

'Kids. Parker, the Gosby constable, says they often walk to school along the old track. He doesn't think the body can have been there long.'

'Where have they taken it? The General?'

'Aye. The PM's at eleven. Either Heinemann or Spenser. I had a quick look. There are no marks.'

'No, I suppose a hole drilled by His Worship the mayor's bullet would have been too much to hope for. Never mind, Bill; you get on with organizing the inquest and I'll send Sergeant Love out to Hambourne. If I hear of any relatives, I'll let you know, but his paper will probably help you there, if you give them a ring.'

Whereupon Inspector Purbright left Sergeant Malley and sought a brief interview with Mr Chubb. He found the chief constable somewhat bewildered.

'They tell me the man died in a booking office, of all places, Mr Purbright. Is that correct?'

'Not quite, sir. Mr Grail's body was *found* in what once had been a booking office.'

'At Hambourne, I understand.'

'Yes, sir. The old Chalmsbury line. He didn't necessarily die there, though.'

'I hope that terrible Scotchman on the council isn't mixed up in this. We'll never hear the end of it.'

Incurring Mr Chubb's displeasure carried the penalty of permanent disqualification from ownership of a name. Alderman Hockley had earned this verbal neutering many years ago by playing a practical joke (he had substituted a fireman's helmet for the chief constable's ceremonial headgear just before an Armistice Day parade, which he regarded as Sassenach mummery) and Mr Chubb had ever since referred to him as 'that Scotchman'.

'I shall make full inquiries, sir, naturally. At the moment we know virtually nothing, so you are quite right to discount speculation as to who might be involved.'

Mr Chubb nodded. 'You'll keep in touch, Mr Purbright, won't you.' And he gave a little wintry smile.

The inspector drove at once to Miriam Lodge. He was admitted by Robert Becket, who led him to the room where Birdie and Lanching were talking to a man in formal morning suit, a long-legged, confident man with a big, handsome head and healthy complexion.

Birdie introduced Sir Arthur Heckington, then said to Purbright: 'How flattering to have you back again so soon, inspector.'

He smiled and sat down, after placing his chair so that he

could see both the girl and the barrister.

Suddenly Birdie put a hand to her mouth in a gesture of contrition. Whether it was real or mocking, Purbright was not sure.

'That message you left for Clive . . .' she said. 'He hasn't rung you, has he? And now you've come to be cross with me.'

'No, he has not rung,' said the inspector, quietly. 'But being cross is not my object in coming here.'

'Oh, goodikins. May I reward you with coffee?'

Purbright took notice neither of the question nor of the laboured coyness with which it was asked. 'Where *is* Mr Grail do you suppose, Miss Clemenceaux?' he asked, in the same gentle tone.

'In London,' she replied simply. 'We've had a call from him.'

The inspector thought he saw a slight shift in the barrister's regard, a warning perhaps; and a tightening of his mouth. Grail, obviously, had been the subject of their conferring.

'When was that call?'

'Last night. Quite late. Possibly after midnight.' She looked at him wonderingly.

'And he sounded as usual, did he? In normal health, and so on?

'Sure. Why, shouldn't he have done?'

A cough, noble as a Wordsworth stanza. Purbright recognized the signal for intervention from the Bar.

'Forgive me, inspector, but may I, also, ask the purport of this line of questioning?'

'You may, Sir Arthur. I am simply seeking elucidation of a problem. If Mr Grail was in good health at around midnight in London, how did he come to be lying dead in a derelict railway station some miles north of Flaxborough eight hours later?'

It took all Heckington's considerable powers of self-possession to field this one. He registered neither surprise nor shock in any visual form, but instead froze in an attitude of keen attention. It was rather like the sudden stopping of a film.

The girl, on the other hand, made no attempt to hide what Purbright felt to be genuine astonishment and dismay. Grief? he wondered. No, not that . . . alarm, rather – a mixture of fright and resentment.

'Clive dead?' she murmured. 'Up here, you say? But he can't

be.' She slowly turned her head and looked at Lanching, then at Becket, as if in appeal.

'At a place called Hambourne, Miss Clemenceaux,' Purbright told her. 'It is on a disused section of railway line. Some boys found Mr Grail's body in the old station building.'

Quickly and unobtrusively, the inspector glanced at the faces of Birdie's companions. Becket's was blank. Lanching looked bewildered but solemn.

Sir Arthur addressed Purbright. 'As I believe you know, inspector, I am retained by the employers of Mr Grail and his colleagues, on behalf of one of whom – Mr Becket – I shall be appearing in your magistrates' court tomorrow. In view of the tragic and, on the face of it, mysterious development of which we have just learned, I am confident that my clients would desire me to act in an advisory capacity during the course of whatever investigations the police deem proper.'

Purbright gave a small bow. 'That seems perfectly reasonable, sir, so long as this lady and the two gentlemen have no objection.'

'No, none,' said Lanching.

Becket shrugged and looked at Birdie. 'I think,' she said, 'that Sir Arthur's advice will be very welcome.'

'May I, then, suggest,' the barrister pressed on without delay, 'that at the outset I have a word in private with our friends so that we may establish the kind of mutual confidence which will be to the advantage of everybody, the police included?'

Purbright rose. Birdie noticed the tendency to stoop, characteristic of a tall man who does a lot of listening to others. 'May I wait in the next room?' he asked her, making it a personal question, addressed to a hostess.

'Of course. I'm sure it will only be for a minute. You must think it awful cheek.'

He smiled at her without comment. From the door, he spoke to the barrister. 'You'll make it brief, will you, sir? There are many inquiries to be made.'

Sir Arthur waited for several seconds after the closing of the door behind Purbright. He adopted a presiding attitude, looked fixedly at each of the others in turn, then spoke with quiet gravity. 'You realize, of course, that Mr Grail's death makes it impossible – indeed, pointless, alas – to contemplate any further negotiation with those responsible for his abduction. This cannot now be regarded as a private matter in any sense. Even if – as I cannot believe – your employers might wish to preserve a position of non-involvement, the law of the land clearly requires them and you to co-operate with the police. I must so advise you now. Furthermore, I must tell you that my own duty lies in helping you to put before that inspector all the facts without further delay.'

There was a pause. Then, just as Sir Arthur made a businesslike movement suggestive of his being about to wind up the proceedings before anyone else could say anything, Becket interposed: 'Hey, that's all very well, but what if these characters never get caught? It's ten to one they won't, and we shall be left holding a damned unpleasant baby. Compounding a felony – isn't that what they call it?'

'There are precedents,' the barrister replied. 'I do not think the director would move without very sympathetic consideration.'

'But we should be liable to prosecution. That's so, isn't it?'

'I cannot add to what I have said already, Miss Clemenceaux. And we really have no choice in the matter.'

She gestured impatiently. 'I don't agree. Nothing need now be said about this kidnapping nonsense. The money no longer enters into it. It can go back.'

Sir Arthur's impeccably groomed eyebrows rose a fraction. 'Nonsense is scarcely a word I expected you to apply to action by people you declared only yesterday to be of homicidal capability.'

'I could have been wrong. This place is packed with eccentrics. Good heavens, they even offer to fight duels. Clive had been challenged, did you know that?'

'My understanding of that affair was that it had been largely contrived for the purposes of publicity,' replied Heckington archly.

'The same argument,' suggested Lanching, 'might be applied to the so-called kidnapping, wouldn't you say?'

'No, Mr Lanching, I should not. A very important point seems to be in some danger of being forgotten. Grail is dead. For all we know, this can now be a murder case.'

Becket who had been leaning forward attentively in his chair, suddenly lounged back. 'Rubbish. He had a heart attack.'

The barrister impaled him with a steely stare. 'I have heard no mention of heart attacks.' He looked round at the others. 'Is there some source of information which I have not yet been privileged to share?'

Birdie answered at once. 'Of course not, Sir Arthur. I think Bob was simply coming out with the obvious assumption.' She smiled. 'We aren't lawyers, you know.'

'Being kidnapped must be extremely frightening,' Lanching said. 'Clive wasn't what I should call fit. These things happen. People collapse.'

Becket made his contribution. 'And what would be the point of killing him before any money's been paid over?'

There was a comparatively long silence. Then Sir Arthur pointed at the door and said: 'I think we might now invite our policeman friend back again.'

Lanching rose to obey.

'I counsel absolute frankness,' said Sir Arthur. 'Most earnestly, I do.'

'And I ask you' – it was Birdie's voice, tense and anxious, while she stared fixedly not at Heckington but at the door which Lanching was about to open – 'not to push us just yet. Not until after the *post mortem*, anyway. One thing you can be sure of. Clive's death was from natural causes. Don't ask me how I know. Take my word, please. If I'm proved wrong – OK, turn everything over and we'll help you. But not immediately. Or there'll be hell to pay, believe me.'

The last few words had been delivered very quietly, but Birdie fancied they were not altogether lost upon the inspector, who entered at that moment rather self-consciously, like a parent inveigled into a game of postman's knock.

He had just sat down when the telephone began to ring. Becket went out. He returned almost at once, and gave the inspector a nod. 'For you.'

As soon as Purbright had left, Heckington turned urgently to Birdie. 'Is there anything you have failed to tell me, Miss Clemenceaux? If so, I beg you not to continue to withhold it.'

For a while she remained silent and seemingly hesitant. Then she shook her head decisively. 'No. Nothing. Nothing at all.'

Sir Arthur gazed at her, his mouth set in a small pout of speculation, one of his most telling courtroom expressions, but she had given no sign of changing her answer by the time Purbright came back into the room and resumed his seat.

'I should like you,' he began, 'to hear first my understanding of what Mr Grail and you – his colleagues, I take it – were doing in Flaxborough. Please correct me if I am wrong. You all were engaged in compiling a newspaper article, or articles, for the *Sunday Herald*, on the subject of films made by local amateur photographers. The films are alleged to be indecent. In short, Mr Grail's job was to expose a scandal, and yours, presumably, to help provide material which would substantiate the story. Would that be a fair summary of why you people came here?'

Becket and Lanching glanced at each other and at Birdie, then shrugged. 'I suppose so,' said Becket.

The girl nodded. 'Yes, that's about it.'

Purbright continued: 'Since your paper's announcement of its intentions, some local people have expressed resentment. I shouldn't imagine that surprised any of you, although' – the inspector smiled faintly – 'a challenge to a duel can scarcely have been expected. Tell me, was Mr Grail upset at all by that?'

'It added to his nervousness, I think,' said Birdie. 'The story hadn't been going well. Clive was a bit tense.'

'What do you mean by not going well, Miss Clemenceaux?'

'Well, on Monday we saw the actual film on which reports had been based. It was not quite what we had been led to expect.'

'It was not indecent, do you mean?'

The girl gave a short, unamused laugh. 'Oh, it was pornographic, all right. In parts. But the whole thing had a doctored look. The story, as it had been accepted up to then, just wouldn't stand up.'

'Yet you are publishing it.'

She shook her head. 'As a matter of fact, we are not. It's being withdrawn.'

Sir Arthur had been regarding Birdie anxiously. He now half raised a hand, as if he was about to intervene.

Purbright watched the hand, but continued to direct his questions to the girl.

'That decision would be a rather serious one for a newspaper, wouldn't it?'

'Very serious. And taken most reluctantly.'

'Would Mr Grail, do you think, have felt himself personally responsible for the failure – if that is the word – of the story? The column did bear his name.'

Birdie considered. 'He certainly was upset. After all, several things had gone wrong. There was Bob's court case' – she looked across at Becket – 'and then the publicity over that silliness of the mayor's. He wasn't terribly fit, you know.'

'Was he not?' The inspector sounded eager to be clear on the point.

'He wasn't, was he,' Birdie appealed to the others in general. Becket and Lanching made gestures of confirmation. Sir Arthur watched them carefully.

'When did you last see Mr Grail?' Purbright asked.

Again, Birdie glanced about her, as if to escape the singularity of the inquisition. 'Yesterday morning,' Lanching volunteered.

'He went out for a walk,' said Becket.

'Did he say where?'

'The housekeeper said she thought he was going to a place called Gosby Vale, wherever that is,' Birdie said. 'Mrs Patmore, she's called. She works for Mr Stamper who owns this house.'

All these names seemed familiar enough to the inspector. 'So Mrs Patmore – as far as you know – was the last person here in the house actually to see Mr Grail?'

'I suppose so, yes.'

'But you did hear from him again.'

'Yes, the call from London . . . well, he *said* he was in London.'

'That doesn't now seem likely, does it, Miss Clemenceaux?'

'I can't imagine why he should have lied.'

Becket leaned forward helpfully. 'We've said he was upset. Overwrought might be more accurate.'

The barrister, who had been preserving a stiff silence, frowned at this interjection.

'Overwrought,' repeated Purbright. He waited a moment. 'Is it your suggestion, sir, that Mr Grail might not have been responsible for his actions?'

'Oh, I don't know about that, but it does seem a possibility, wouldn't you say?'

The inspector regarded Becket with an expression of newly

aroused, but polite, interest. 'By the way, in what field do *you* operate for the paper, sir?'

'I'm a photographer. A free-lance, actually, but the *Herald* commission me to do particular features from time to time.'

'I see,' said the inspector, pleasantly. 'Tell me – I'm not familiar with the workings of journalism – is a photographer chosen on account of some special qualification? Knowledge of the subject, say. Or of the district in question.'

Becket smiled. 'Not as a rule. An editor assumes that the honour of working for his paper opens all minds as well as all doors.'

'Ah . . . So I mustn't get the idea that you – or any of your three colleagues – was chosen for this assignment by virtue of your having previously worked or lived in the area?'

'No, you mustn't, because that would be quite wrong.'

Purbright glanced down at some notes he had been making, then thoughtfully rubbed his right forefinger with three fingers of the left hand. He surveyed, one by one, the three journalists and the barrister.

'I think it is only fair to tell you,' he said, 'that the phone call I received a few minutes ago was from the acting police surgeon, Doctor Spenser, and that he had something disturbing to tell me. It appears from his preliminary examination of the body that Grail's death was not from natural causes, but that in all likelihood he died from some form of poisoning.'

The ensuing silence was broken by the portentous sound – a kind of laryngeal fanfare – of Sir Arthur's preparation for an important statement.

'It is quite clear,' the barrister began, 'from what you have just said, inspector, that my clients are now under mandatory obligation to reveal certain facts which loyalty to their employers had previously prevented them from making public. They will wish me, I know, to set forth those facts without further delay, in the hope that they may be of aid to the police in their inquiries.

'Firstly, Mr Grail did not – as might have been thought natural – simply wander away while under strain and ultimately find himself in London. He *did* go for a walk yesterday morning, certainly, but no one knows where that walk ended. And he *did* speak to his colleagues by telephone at about midnight, but by then he was acting not so much under strain as under duress.'

'Duress,' repeated Purbright, flatly.

'Not to put too fine a point on it,' said the barrister, 'he was being held prisoner. The first indication of this had come in the form of telephoned demands – at about seven in the evening, wasn't it, Miss Clemenceaux?' (Yes, she said, just before seven.) 'And there was, in fact, a meeting of a kind. All this you will doubtless wish to be put on record as detailed statements by my clients.'

'That would seem to be indicated, yes.'

If Sir Arthur recognized in Purbright's urbane manner a rebuke of his own case-hogging propensities, he made no remark upon it. Instead, he hooked one elegantly tailored arm over the rail of his chair, crossed his legs, and leaned back as if in confident expectation of a vote of thanks.

Purbright looked at the others. 'Two or three of my officers will be here shortly,' he announced. 'When they arrive, your statements will be taken. I should also appreciate co-operation during whatever searching of the house we may consider necessary. Miss Clemenceaux – should the telephone ring, will you please answer it just as if we weren't here.'

It was nearly half an hour later that an opportunity occurred for Birdie to vent her feelings in private. She was in the kitchen making coffee when Lanching entered with an offer to help carry the eight cups.

'And now what the hell do we do? That bloody old woman of a lawyer! What a great performance he's put up. We'd just about managed to ditch Grail's unstuck plot when along comes that idiot to hand it back to us. Kidnappers and all. Christikins, it's too bloody much, it really is.'

Lanching watched her carry the kettle from the stove and jet boiling water savagely into the cups. 'It's certainly made things difficult,' he said.

Birdie wrenched open the door of the refrigerator and stood staring, not seeing at first the bottle of milk that confronted her. 'Difficult!' she echoed, bitterly.

Lanching pointed to the milk. 'I got the impression,' he said, 'rightly or wrongly, that that inspector wasn't buying the kidnap story, anyway.'

She turned and stared at him. 'Why ever not, for God's sake?'

'It could be,' said Lanching, 'that he's one of those people who aren't as stupid as newspapers would like them to be.'

Chapter Fifteen

THE INQUIRIES INTO THE DEATH OF CLIVE GRAIL WERE IN the charge of Detective Inspector Purbright, acting on behalf of the chief constable, Mr Harcourt Chubb. He was assisted by Detective Sergeant Sidney Love; Sergeant William Malley, coroner's officer; three officers in plain clothes, named Harper, Pook and Hollis; and five uniformed constables. Subsidiary and specialized aid was provided by the East Midlands Forensic Science department; the Post Office; the acting police surgeon and the pathology department of Flaxborough General Hospital. Co-operation on less formal levels was forthcoming from Josiah Kebble, editor of the *Flaxborough Citizen*; from Chung Lee Ha, restaurant proprietor; and from an old gentleman in Brocklestone-on-Sea who remembered the making of a cinematograph record of that resort's Armistice celebration in 1918.

Subsequent, and vitally important, information was to come from a draper, a garage proprietor and a murderer, with degrees of reluctance in that order.

The actual process of investigation might have appeared to the casual observer to be neither urgent nor sequential.

Soon after nine o'clock on that Wednesday morning, Sergeant Love and a man with a camera and a case of equipment arrived by car at Hambourne station. Two constables in uniform were already standing outside the building.

Love rubbed his hands and glanced about him with a heavily judicious expression until one of the uniformed men tapped his arm and pointed out some marks on the ground. Love stared at the marks, frowned, stroked his lower lip for a few moments, then nodded gravely and indicated that the photographer might record them for higher authority. When that had been done, the sergeant made some measurements.

They moved into the station's entrance hall and surveyed the rubble-strewn floor and disfigured walls. In a broken frame, the attractions of the sea front at Great Yarmouth were commemorated by a poster of two children with buckets and spades and beards. The beards, together with a speech balloon inscribed 'Aggy Hall has big tits', appeared to have been added later.

In a room adjoining the hallway, an irregularly shaped space on the ground was marked out in white tape. The photographer took a shot of it in relation to its surroundings, then another in close-up. Love had a long look round. He picked up various small objects, examined them, and dropped a selection into an envelope. The glances he directed at the photographer from time to time were at first portentous, then inscrutable. Neither kind drew response. 'You'd think he was working for a different firm,' the sergeant was later to complain to Malley.

Purbright's direction of inquiries at the house proceeded fairly smoothly until mid-morning, when Mrs Lily Patmore appeared at the kitchen door. Loyalty to Farmer Stamper, combined with a delicious intuition of something odd going on, had overweighed sisterly concern and put her on the 11.15 bus.

At the sight of Detective Constable Hollis methodically pillaging the waste bin, Mrs Patmore swelled with indignation and demanded what the hell he thought he was sossing about with. Hollis said she would have to put such questions to the inspector, and very soon the housekeeper found herself seated in confidential company with a man who was actually interested in what she had to say instead of forever awming twixt arse and tit.

Though unaware of having been compared so favourably with Farmer Stamper, Purbright learned a number of things about the house's tenants in transit. There had been quarrels, for instance: not of deadly seriousness, perhaps, but the sort that suggest permanent underlying mistrust. He heard of a picture show behind a closed bedroom door and attended by men old enough to be that girl's father and respectable enough, one might have thought, to know better. A big London lawyer, for instance, and that fat, white-haired little gentleman who was the editor of the *Citizen*. He was informed also of a room kept locked upstairs (she indicated which one) that was supposed to have valuable equipment in it. Valuable it might be, added Mrs Patmore, but if it hadn't blown its nose when she was passing the door on the way to her own room she was very much mistaken. Then there was poor Mr Grail's interest in Harry Pearce, the draper (what might a famous newspaper writer want to meet *him* for, for heaven's sake?) and in the garage man, Alf Blossom, who was to be trusted about half as far as some of his hire cars could be driven.

Purbright listened and made notes and looked as if Mrs Patmore's arrival was the nicest thing that had happened to him on that or any other day.

By this time, Sergeant Malley had piloted the coroner through the formalities of opening and adjourning the inquest. He emerged, wheezing, from his old car at almost the same moment as Love's arrival at Miriam Lodge. They joined Purbright in the plastic annexe that Farmer Stamper's builder had assured him was the conservatory. It was hot and stuffy, but secure from eavesdropping.

'When can we expect the autopsy report, Bill?' Purbright asked.

Malley mistrustfully lowered himself into a canvas chair. He unfastened the top two buttons of his trousers and considered. 'All the obvious things, he'll let us have in the next hour or two, I should think. We'll have to wait longer for the clever stuff.'

'Spenser's fairly confident that the man was poisoned, though, isn't he?'

'Oh, aye,' said Malley, equably. 'Something cyanic and pretty quick.' He delved into a pouch of tobacco, and Purbright saw that a short, black pipe was in his fist. 'Stomach contents were obvious as a menu, apparently. He must just have eaten.'

The inspector nodded. 'That could be helpful, but it's *where* he ate that we'd like to know.' He turned to Love. 'How did you get on, Sid?'

Love was standing a little apart, looking expectantly through a plastic pane in the direction from which he had come. He spoke over his shoulder. 'I can tell you better in half a minute. Harper's getting a measurement for me. We didn't want to look obvious.'

'Quite right, Sid,' Purbright commended. He had just seen Detective Constable Harper come round the corner of the house. Harper was reeling in a huge tape measure as he walked; he looked like a tuna fisherman in difficulties.

Love went out to confer with Harper. On his return, he gave the inspector a meaningful smirk. 'Tyres,' he said, carelessly. 'Track width. It all matches up.'

Purbright conferred upon Love an impressed 'Ah' in the manner of a trainer presenting a lump of sugar. 'I thought it might,' he added. Looking slightly perplexed, Malley ambled out.

Soon afterwards, there came a tap on the annexe door. One of the plain clothes men put his head round.

'Come in, Mr Hollis.'

'I've been down to that Chinky takeaway, sir.' Hollis was of the persuasion that Chinese restaurants were dedicated in the main to opium smoking and the dissection of cats.

'And?'

'I had a job to find anybody I could get any sense out of, but in the end the boss's daughter got back from school to have her dinner and it turned out she could speak more or less proper English so there was me asking questions and her being a sort of interpreter like and everything went great – at least the Chinks keep books, if you can call them that, and they remembered there was only one order last night that would have needed eight containers so one of them turned up the record and it was something they just called "E", the letter "E", E for elephant, and to them it means dinner for four people, and I've got a description here of what goes in it, and it sounds a pretty weird lot of rubbish, and all. Sir.'

'At what time,' the inspector asked, 'was this meal collected?'

'They thought about ten o'clock, sir.'

'Could they give any description of the person who came? Or persons?'

'There was only one, they thought. A woman. "Nice lady" they kept calling her, but perhaps they just thought that was being co-operative. I couldn't get a proper description out of them.'

Purbright gave a little smile. 'These English ladies, they all look the same, you know, Mr Hollis.'

Hollis looked worried. 'I wouldn't have thought so, sir.'

Purbright sent him to seek out and request the attendance, as soon as it might be convenient, of retired draper Henry Pearce.

'Are our reluctant guests all managing to occupy their time pleasantly?' Purbright asked Love.

The sergeant was about to reply when he caught sight of a figure looming up to the door. 'Here's one who isn't,' he murmured.

Sir Arthur Heckington entered. 'You will forgive my intrusion, inspector,' he declared, with absolute confidence.

Purbright smiled thinly.

'I wish my clients to overlook nothing which might be of assistance in getting to the bottom of this highly regrettable affair. There does exist a tape recording. Are you aware of this tape recording, Purbright?'

The inspector said he was not, but there had not yet been time for all the relevant facts to be marshalled. He would see that the recording was not overlooked.

'Then, of course, there is the question of the film,' said Sir Arthur. It sounded like reference by a conscientious guardian to some mad and singularly unsavoury relative.

'You've seen the film, have you, sir?'

'I admit to that dubious privilege.'

'Is there anything about it to which you feel you should draw my attention?'

The barrister reflected briefly before replying. 'No – that is what I find somewhat perplexing, and my clients have been unable to clarify the issue. You see, those sections of the film involving local people are perfectly innocuous records of public occasions. The sound-track, as I am led to understand, is itself indecent, but of course it has been added later. So have certain all-too-explicit displays of concupiscence by anonymous – indeed, unidentifiable – performers.'

'You say that the pornographic parts of the film are not contributed by local people, but how can you be sure if those taking part are not identifiable?'

Heckington frowned deeply. He clearly did not care to be on the receiving end of cross-examination.

'Too professional, my dear man. Altogether too professional.'

'I see, sir.' Purbright forbore from asking Sir Arthur to cite his credentials in this delicate field of judgment. He suggested instead that such facts made it less easy to ascribe Grail's kidnapping to outraged local opinion.

Heckington, QC, concurred.

'I am far from happy,' he went on, 'about this abduction, or whatever it was. My clients I must own to be intelligent, talented and by no means naïve young people; but are they, I ask myself, proof against the machinations of the publishing world? Nearly all of us, alas, inspector, are capable of being misled, if only for a very short time.'

Purbright noted in this declaration of the general principle of human frailty the insertion of a typical Heckington personal escape clause. Blandly, he repeated it. 'Ah, yes, sir. *Nearly* all of us.'

'I have represented newspaper interests long enough,' Sir Arthur continued, unabashed, 'to know that there is no limit to the extremities wherewith rival claims are promoted. This could be just such an instance. After all, the story *has* been suppressed – or so I am assured – and corresponding damage has been done to the reputation of the *Herald*. For such a result, the unorthodox and unlawful means might well have been considered worthwhile by some.'

'Including a man's death?' Purbright asked, softly.

'Ah, as to that, I fancy that it will be found that the element of pure coincidence has – most unfortunately – entered this sad story, inspector. Food-poisoning is an ever-present menace in these times.'

Purbright changed the subject. 'Would there be any objection on your part – or on Mr Becket's, perhaps I should say – to a further adjournment of his driving case tomorrow, sir? It would seem to be a diversion we all could do without at the moment.'

Sir Arthur puffed his cheeks in a picture of amiable compliance. 'But of course, my dear Purbright; I agree absolutely.' A short pause for rapid thought. 'I do not doubt but that when this somewhat trivial case does come before the court, the prosecution will offer a quid pro quo in respect of my client's inconvenience . . .' The eloquent brows rose like inverted scales of justice.

'Who knows?' replied the inspector ('Very dry, is my boss,' Love had more than once informed his young lady).

The re-installed Mrs Patmore was preparing lunch for all but policemen. Her employer, who was nothing if not a naturally inquisitive man, had called to make himself one of the number in order to observe from a position of privilege the conduct of a criminal investigation. What he had not reckoned upon, perhaps, was the possibility of his being questioned himself, so when a constable appeared to conduct him into the presence of Inspector Purbright, Farmer Stamper's visage set at once, like concrete, into those lines of rural intransigence which town dwellers erroneously suppose to proclaim the half-wit.

Purbright's opening was gently malicious. 'Nice house, Herbert. The missus must be pleased with it.'

'Suits me.'

'Sort of lodgers, are they, these London people?'

'Ah.'

'The one who died. Know anything about him?'

'Know nowt about any of 'em.'

The inspector scratched an ear lazily. 'Mr Grail, though – you'd done some asking around to oblige him.'

'Oh, ah?'

'A couple of names. Harry Pearce – was that one?'

'Could've been. Who says?'

'I forget now. It just came up. They do, you know, Bert.'

'He was interested in photography. Grail was.'

'So I believe. What about Alf, though?'

'Alf?'

'Alf Blossom. At the garage on the South Circuit.'

'No idea. I did wonder.'

'Anyone have it in for Grail, do you think? Anyone round here?'

'No. Why should they?'

'As you say, why should they. Right, then, Bert – you'll be wanting to go down for a look at your beet. Hey – by God, but have you seen old Mawksley's?'

The stone face cracked at last. 'Aye, I bloody have. By Christ, he came arse uppards with that bloody lot, didn't he?'

'By Christ, he did.'

Stamper paused at the door. 'That mucky film,' he said, casually. 'I reckon you might be wasting your time talking to Harry Pearce.'

'Oh, aye?'

'Aye. You could have a word with Joss Kebble, though. About his number plate.' With which enigmatic suggestion, Mr

Stamper slammed his conservatory door behind him and wandered in the direction of the kitchen.

'What on earth did he mean by that?' asked Love, who had been listening to the conversation between inspector and witness with growing disapproval.

'I don't know, Sid,' said Purbright, 'but I think it falls into the category of what Sir Arthur calls a quid pro quo.'

Chapter Sixteen

PURBRIGHT RETURNED TO POLICE HEADQUARTERS IN FEN Street shortly before four o'clock. He was on his own. He wished to make a telephone call to London and to enjoy at the same time the slightly corroborant effect of police station tea that he felt would be helpful during a conversation with the kind of man who gets appointed to the managing editorship of the *Sunday Herald*.

Richardson granted him audience without demur, but wanted to know why the inspector could not address his questions to Sir Arthur Heckington, the man on the spot.

'Because I seriously doubt if he could answer them, sir. The matter is of some urgency – and possibly of delicacy, also. I need the co-operation of a person in authority.'

'And you're called, what? Purbright? Purbright – is that right?'

'That is so, Mr Richardson. Detective inspector is my rank, and I am in charge of the inquiries into the sudden death of Mr Clive Grail.'

'Grail ... y-e-e-s ...' Richardson dragged out the word dubiously, as if unwilling to reveal that the *Sunday Herald* was about to decide that Grail had never existed. Then he seemed to give a start. 'Delicacy? What's this about delicacy?'

'Let me explain, sir. I do know something of the nature of the story that Mr Grail and his colleagues were working on. And it is my understanding that the original information – the tip-off, I suppose one should call it – came from someone in this locality.

'I recognize a newspaper's desire to protect its sources of information, and it is in this context that I have used the word delicacy. You see, I believe a link may exist between Mr Grail's informant and whatever caused his death. It is most important that this person be identified. And as quickly as possible.'

There was silence at the Fleet Street end. Purbright supposed the managing editor to be grappling with the ethical implications he had raised. In fact, Richardson was moving a poised forefinger along a row of multi-coloured buttons on a desk console while he peered, hang-jawed, at their identifying tags. At last he found the one he wanted and jabbed it.

A voice, boxed and catarrhal. 'Features.'

Richardson spoke. 'Grail's village blue movie story. What source?'

'Hang on.'

The answer, such as it was, came two minutes later.

'As far as we can make out, Grail was handling it pretty much on his own. A Middle East staffman ran an actual copy of the flick to earth, I believe, but only because he was asked to.'

'There'd be payment,' Purbright heard Richardson say. 'Check authorizations round that time. The cashier will have a record.'

The inspector, given Richardson's promise of a call back within the next half hour or so, prepared to use the interval as profitably as its brevity allowed. He rang the *Flaxborough Citizen* office and asked Mr Kebble if he would be so kind as to spare a few minutes. The editor assured him that nothing would give him greater pleasure; he forthwith donned his large, Citizen Kane-style hat, and thankfully abandoned his least favourite task of the week, the subbing of a clutch of wedding reports.

Mr Kebble knew his way to the inspector's office on the first floor. As a billiards player always ready to accommodate himself to policemen's unsociable hours and as an amiable and trustworthy gossip, he was already a familiar visitor to Fen Street and welcomed by all but the most misanthropic of its inmates.

'You will have heard, no doubt,' Purbright said to him, once the spherical editor had been settled, beamingly attentive, behind a mug of tea, 'what has happened to your distinguished colleague from London.'

Mr Kebble's expression changed instantly to one of grave solicitude. 'They tell me,' he said, 'the poor chap's been found dead.'

'Out at Hambourne, yes. Odd place to be. You've no ideas on the subject, have you, Joss? Anyone said anything?'

'Not a word, old chap.'

'What does your friend Barry Hoole think about Grail?'

Kebble smiled mournfully. 'As a duellist, not much.'

Purbright, too, looked amused, but the questions kept coming. 'Was that just one of Charlie Hockley's larger lunacies, or did something lie behind it, do you think?'

'Oh, I don't think so.' Wistfully, 'Nice little story, though.'

'The duel, do you mean? Or the indecent film? They tell me you were lucky enough to be at the première, Joss.'

Kebble had extracted from one of his waistcoat pockets a tiny, pearl-handled penknife, with which he now was putting the finishing touches to a pencil point. Chin tucked into chest, he interspersed speech with the gentle puffs and snorts that, for him, constituted breathing.

'God, aye,' acknowledged Mr Kebble. 'Never seen anything like it, old chap. Shouldn't think even you have.'

Purbright thanked him for his good opinion. 'I still have the film to look forward to,' he said, 'but I'd be interested to know now if anyone with local connections is involved.'

The editor looked up. 'Dozens,' he declared.

'No – in the indecent parts, I mean. The impression I was given is that the thing is a compilation, a sort of hotch-potch with a linking commentary.'

'Aye, that's right. The funny thing is this, though – this fellow and his tottie who provide all the acrobatics seem to be doing a kind of take-off of characters in the local operatic society.'

'That must have been a refreshing change,' Purbright remarked. Kebble went into a positive eruption of chuckles, in the midst of which he suddenly raised a finger.

'I'll tell you something very odd about that film, old chap.' Kebble leaned forward confidentially and set the finger to work stroking his chin. 'I can't understand it at all, but I'm sure I wasn't mistaken. It was while this pair were going through their all-in wrestling act.'

Purbright signified with a nod that he was paying attention.

'The lighting had been arranged so that their faces couldn't be seen,' went on Kebble. 'The background was dark, but there did

135

seem to be curtains there. Curtains, or sheets of dark cloth, hanging down. And this is what's queer.

'In one corner, low down, and just for a few seconds, I could see a number. It was dim, but I could definitely make it out.' The editor glanced at the door and leaned even closer. 'And do you know why I remember it now?'

The inspector refrained from spoiling such a moment. 'No,' he said, simply.

'It was my own car number, old chap! That's why.'

There was a pause.

'On the screen, do you mean – projected on it?' Purbright asked.

'Yes.'

'When I say projected, I'm thinking of the way a car number is superimposed on a cinema screen for a moment when the owner is being asked to move the car.'

Seeing the point, Mr Kebble shook his head vigorously. 'No, no, not like that. This had got into the film at the time. The actual number plate. OFW 532.'

'Front plate or rear?'

Mr Kebble thought a few seconds. 'Rear – it was more square-shaped.'

'Did you see nothing of the car itself, Joss? I take it you don't suggest the plate had been detached specially – as some sort of kinky prop, perhaps?'

'Do you remember old Alderman Dray at Chalmsbury?' asked Mr Kebble, tempted into irrelevance. 'Dicky had eight daughters, all ugly. Old Dick always turned up for council meetings before anybody else. They reckoned it was the ram's horn snuffbox on the mayor's table that had an erotic fascination for him. He was never spotted at it, mind, but there wasn't one councillor in Chalmsbury who would accept a pinch of snuff from that horn.'

Purbright steered the conversation out of the pleasurable back-waters of the editor's reminiscence into a narrower channel. 'If – as it seems reasonable to suppose – the number plate was in its normal position at the time, can you think of an explanation of how your car came to be in the background during the making of a pornographic film?'

If Mr Kebble admitted to his mind the possibility that a clever and determined policeman might seek to implicate him as an accessory to scandalous crime, he clearly did not suspect Purbright of any such intention. 'I should think,' he said, lamely, after consideration, 'that it just happened to be around and somebody chucked a cover over it.'

'More than likely,' said the inspector.

The telephone rang. It was Richardson. Purbright listened to what he had to say and made some notes. He put a couple of supplementary questions but drew nothing worth noting down. To Mr Kebble, he apologized for the interruption.

'That's all right, old chap. I've been thinking.'

'Good. About places where your car might have been left on its own in the last year or so?'

'Aye.' Kebble frowned. He was palm-rolling a pencil. 'Any idea of a likely date?'

'None. How long have you had the car?'

'Oh . . . three, nearly four years.'

'Do you have it serviced?'

'When it's asthma gets bad. Not regularly.'

'Where?'

'Tom Nicholson does it.'

The inspector shook his head. 'I can't see Tom as Flax's Cecil B. de Mille. Anyway, his place wouldn't be big enough.'

For a while, Purbright stared absently at Mr Kebble's hat, which still reposed on the back of its owner's head. When he spoke again, it was in the manner of delivering a casual afterthought. 'Tell me, Joss – did you ever have anything done to your wagon by South Circuit Motors?'

A gleam shone suddenly in Mr Kebble's eye. 'You're right, old chap. I did. They took it in for a fortnight last year to fit a new cylinder head. August, I should think.'

'Mr Blossom,' said Purbright, 'has pretty extensive premises, with that showroom next to the service bay. It must ease his problems when cars under repair have to be kept there for a few days.'

The editor knew better than to push speculation too far. He changed the subject. 'They tell me there'll be another adjournment of Becket's driving case tomorrow.'

Purbright confirmed that this was so. He found himself wondering why the worldly-wise Kebble should mention a matter of such relative triviality. Then he saw that the man wore the expression of amused mystification which he recognized as a portent of confidence-sharing.

'Funny thing about that case,' remarked Mr Kebble. 'It's about as serious as farting on a Sunday, yet Grail's tottie went to the trouble of coming in specially to talk to me about it.'

'To try and have it kept out of the paper, you mean?'

'Aye – well, that's what it amounted to, although she was fly enough to wrap it up as some sort of professional favour.'

Purbright considered. 'Why do *you* think they didn't want the case to get into print?'

'I don't know, but it's odd. A journalist wouldn't dream of trying that on unless there was the hell of a lot at stake. These people aren't even near home. Why should they worry about local publicity?'

'*Local* publicity?'

'Aye. It was the Flaxborough paper the girl was bothered about. And then only for the next couple of weeks – you know, as if they wanted to be out of the area before names got around.'

Purbright frowned. 'But everyone knew they were here – and why. Their own paper had already seen to that.'

Mr Kebble agreed that the motive for Miss Clemenceaux's approach was difficult to guess. 'One thing you can be sure of, though, old chap – she's not likely to tell you if she doesn't want to.'

The inspector had only one more question to put to the editor of the *Flaxborough Citizen*, and he had little hope of its proving productive. 'Do you happen to remember,' he asked, 'a man called Henry Bush? In his early thirties. Something of a philanderer, I believe. His wife died of poisoning.'

Mr Kebble diligently rolled his pencil. 'I remember the woman's death,' he said. 'It was a damn good story. That was before I came to Flax, though. I tell you who *would* be able to tell you about him – or about her, rather. Bush was supposed to have skipped off with another tottie some time before his missus died. Have a word with Harry Pearce. He's a councillor. Used to keep a draper's shop, they tell me.'

At Miriam Lodge, Purbright remarked to Love on the way in which Pearce's name kept cropping up. The man himself had now done so, announced Love, with the air of a successful conjuror: Hollis had brought him in nearly half an hour ago.

'I really must apologize,' said the inspector to the stringy, narrow-headed, humourless-looking man whom he found waiting nervously in a room on his own, 'for keeping you so long. It was good of you to come.'

'In point of fact, and actually,' said Mr Pearce, 'I was brought.'

Purbright smiled reassuringly. He remembered Pearce now in connection with two events. As one was a murder trial and the other an inquest, the possibility occurred to him that the man might be beginning to regard himself as investigation-prone.

'Oh, not brought, Mr Pearce – or only in the narrowest sense of your being afforded transport.'

'As I understood matters, I was being asked to help the police with their inquiries, but nobody has said what inquiries.' Councillor Pearce followed up this slightly plaintive observation with a thoughtful silence, then said suddenly and to no purpose that Purbright could imagine: 'With respect.'

'A gentleman named Clive Grail – a journalist from London – has died suddenly while on a visit to Flaxborough, Mr Pearce. Hence the inquiries you mention. Were you acquainted with Mr Grail, sir?'

'The answer to that must be no. Definitely no.'

Purbright looked surprised. 'But he was anxious to talk to you, or so I have been told by more than one person. It seems you shared a common interest.'

'Am I allowed to know *what* interest, officer?'

'Of course you are, sir. Photography. And you really have no need to be defensive. No one has thought of accusing you of anything.'

Pearce looked as if he was about to dispute this. Then he turned his head aside and stared, in mute martyrdom, at the empty fireplace.

'Having regard to photography,' he said, 'I don't suppose that the point about me being secretary of the Cine Society is in dispute, and so I rest it where it stands.'

Undismayed by the imponderables of Mr Pearce's council

debating style, the inspector tried a straight question. 'As secretary, did you ever hear it suggested that certain members of the club might be concerned in making films on the side – the sort of films that the general membership would not have approved of?'

'Never,' declared Mr Pearce. 'Very definitely, never.'

'So, Mr Grail would have been wasting his time if he had come to see you in hope of your confirming the truth of such stories?'

'His time and mine.'

Purbright nodded, then, without pause, added: 'You were acquainted, of course, with Mr and Mrs Henry Bush, at the time when they both were active members of the club?'

'Now, look here, inspector . . .' Pearce had half-raised a hand, as if to ward off an assault. For an instant, Purbright saw actual alarm in his eyes. He pressed his advantage.

'Would it surprise you, Mr Pearce, to learn that it was Bush who gave Clive Grail the information on which the *Sunday Herald* decided to base a story about pornographic filming in Flaxborough?'

'By God, *he* had room to talk!'

Too late did Pearce realize that his venting of long-suppressed anger and disgust had also let out what this policeman would see at once as a highly suggestive accusation.

'By which,' said Purbright, 'I take you to mean that Bush was involved in precisely the sort of activity the *Herald* wished to investigate.'

'You can take me to mean that the man you're talking about had an evil mind and evil ways,' Pearce retorted sulkily.

'Did you know he had made approaches to the paper?'

'For money?' Pearce made the phrase sound like the entire Judas story.

'Oh, yes; for money, certainly.'

'So I had heard.'

'Had others heard, Mr Pearce?'

'I suppose so. Some of them had telephone calls from the paper. They were pestering calls.'

'Do you know if Mrs Bush ever received such a call?'

Again anger flared; it seemingly was an emotion that Pearce found difficult to control before it could set off an indiscretion.

'Do *I* know? Never mind if *I* know. *You* know, all right. Why else would you be asking me all this? Why else should poor Edie have . . .' The sentence tailed into bitter, recriminatory silence.

For some moments, Purbright regarded Pearce thoughtfully. When he spoke, it was quite without overtones of blame or suspicion. 'I can recall nothing being said at the inquest on Mrs Bush about her having been subjected to inquiries from a newspaper.'

Pearce said nothing.

'And yet,' the inspector went on, 'she must have been receiving them not very long before the accident.'

Again Pearce made no reply.

Purbright shifted his long frame into a more relaxed posture in his chair. 'Tell me, Mr Pearce – you seem to have known Edith Bush fairly well – how did she come to marry a man who showed so little concern for her?'

It looked at first as if Pearce had settled into sullen uncommunicativeness. Then Purbright saw the thin hands unclench, the shoulders droop within the rusty black Sunday-best jacket into which the draper's wife had insistently thrust him for his outing in a police car, and the sad, watery eyes rise to meet his own. It's what he wants, thought Purbright. Talking about her. It's what he wants.

'He was rubbish,' declared Pearce, 'but she was infatuated with him. He could make her do anything he wanted. I don't know where he turned up from. Not from round here. And not from Brocklestone, either.'

'Brocklestone?'

'Brocklestone was Edie's home. She came here after her father died and got a job with Fieldings Photographic. That's where he met her, as I understand it. He made out he was some sort of fashion photographer. Before many weeks were out, he'd put paid to her self-respect.' Pearce gave the inspector a long, meaningful stare. 'They co-habited.'

Purbright had the feeling he was expected to register profound shock. He did his best with a soundless whistle. It made him look momentarily nonchalant. 'They did marry, though, surely?'

'Oh, yes,' agreed Pearce, with heavy irony, 'they locked the stable door.'

'But it was not a happy marriage.'

Pearce pondered the proposition as if the word 'happy' had never before occurred to him in a matrimonial context. Then, 'He debauched her,' he declared with finality.

'In what way, Mr Pearce?'

'I would rather not say.'

Purbright sighed. 'Look sir, I'm not sure if you appreciate the object of the questions we are now asking you – among others. A man is dead. The circumstances of his death are odd, to put it mildly. I think now that two earlier deaths may not be unrelated. So long as the facts remain obscure, there must be a danger of further violence. You can help prevent this happening, but only by giving frank answers.'

'I've been as frank as I can. As my conscience permits.'

'That is not my impression, Mr Pearce.'

'Never mind your impressions, officer. There is a right and a wrong way of going about these things. Why don't you ask the man Bush about what he made his wife do, if you're so interested?'

'Because,' said Purbright, 'the man Bush happens to have been killed. His was one of the earlier deaths I mentioned just now.'

The statement was made quietly, almost casually, but there was alertness and calculation in the inspector's eye. He did not miss Pearce's quick intake of breath. What he was not prepared for, though, was the draper's immediate seizure of his arm and the hoarsely whispered demand:

'*Did they get the one who did it?*'

Chapter Seventeen

THE PROPRIETOR OF THE SOUTH CIRCUIT GARAGE HAD A manner exactly suitable to the fleeting nature of most of his commercial transactions. He was a breezy man. And Mr Alfred Blossom's breeziness would intensify in ratio to the questionableness of the deal in hand at the moment.

Policemen inspired him to a positive gale of facetious good fellowship.

To Purbright and Love he offered in quick succession a handshake, the eye-winking hope that they knew better than to look for any knocked-off wagons on *his* premises, and an invitation to drink what he called 'some special sherry wine' in his office.

The inspector, whose single experience of Mr Blossom's hospitality had left an impression vaguely suggestive of anti-freeze, explained regretfully that they both were on duty. Mr Blossom laughed in the back of his nose. 'That's right, matey. Yes, matey. Gorblimey-O'Reilly!'

Love smiled in sympathy with the roguishness of the jolly car dealer. 'Bit of a card, this one,' he whispered to Purbright, as they crossed the court behind Blossom.

'Yes, Sid,' the inspector said.

They climbed some stairs and entered a prefabricated cabin containing two big desks and some comfortable office chairs on plain but good quality carpet. There were typewriters, an elaborate looking calculator and a filing system that contrived to embody a buzzer and coloured lights. The heat was considerable. On the walls hung six calendars, presented by tyre and accessory factors; each pictured a near-nude in some unlikely situation.

'We should be obliged,' Purbright opened, 'if you could tell us when a particular car was brought in here for repair.'

Mr Blossom leered delightedly at each in turn. 'All in the records, matey.' He swept an arm towards the filing cabinet. 'Everything's there. All the lot. God-alive-o.'

The inspector gave Blossom the registration number of Josiah Kebble's car and his address.

'That's all I need matey. Everything's here. This is how we do it. God-alive-o.'

And Blossom delved amidst the keys and fairy-lights of the filing system. A minute later, he emerged, his little pink eyes puckered with exasperation behind their pebble lenses. He shook his head. 'I don't know, matey. You'd think they could use a simple thing like that without ballsing it up. Hang on, I'll fetch Jenny. Blimey-O'Reilly.'

The girl who appeared in response to Blossom's summons was his secretary. Hers was the look of patiently borne suffering that successive relays of staff at the South Circuit Garage carried as a testimonial to their employer and a warning to their own prospective successors.

Jenny produced the relevant card without trouble, and left

immediately. The inspector noticed that she automatically kept a fixed distance from Blossom.

'Hand-picked, my staff is, matey. Hand-picked. No rubbish.'

Purbright was looking at the card. 'It appears from this that Mr Kebble's car was on these premises during the first week of September, last year, sir.'

'Does it, matey? Yes, well, it must have been, then. If that says so.'

For a moment, the inspector treated Mr Blossom to a regard of trusting earnestness, rather as one might expose meat to infra-red rays to render it more edible.

'I feel sure,' he said, 'that I can safely take you into our confidence regarding a matter which I admit has nothing to do with the motor trade.'

'Do you, matey? God-alive-o. Yes, I reckon so. Just you carry on.' And Blossom assumed an expression of solicitude that would have added fifty pounds to any car in his stock.

'What I want you to tell me about that period early last September, sir, concerns not car repairs but films.' And Purbright, anxious not to promote association of ideas, tried to avoid looking at any of the calendars.

'Films, matey?' The fishbowl magnification of Blossom's blue eyes behind the thick lenses was quite steady.

'I know, of course, that you're a member of the Photographic Society, and that you help where you can to provide your fellow members with indoor facilities.'

'Ah. You know that, do you, matey? That's all right, then.' The facetiousness had an edge of challenge not quite in keeping with Blossom's fixed grin.

'Oh, perfectly all right, Mr Blossom. I should think a cleared showroom would make an excellent studio for private film-making.'

'Should you, matey? I wouldn't know.'

From Purbright, a long, reassuring smile. 'You know, Alf, you're wasted in this corrupt and mechanized age. It is too sophisticated, too devious for you. You are a natural-born horse trader. May we now deal on that basis?'

Nothing flattered Mr Blossom more surely than an implication of villainousness. His grin suddenly became one of real pleasure;

he lowered his head in a curiously diffident attitude, like a bird seeking shelter beneath its own wing; he closed his eyes and simultaneously raised his brows; and protested, in even more adenoidal tones than usual: 'I don't know what you mean, matey. Taking it out of me again, I suppose, matey. God alive-o. Don't know what you're on about. God alive-o, matey.'

Sergeant Love stared in his perplexity first at Blossom, then at Purbright, but both men appeared to find the exchange perfectly natural.

'What I wish to know,' the inspector was now saying to Blossom, 'is pretty urgent from my point of view, so I shall offer the favours first. One: no fuss to be made about unauthorized use of premises where a special fire risk exists. Two: I propose to accept that the head of a respectable and long-established automobile business would not knowingly be associated with the making of pornographic films, let alone take any of the profits.'

Blossom signified by a prolonged nasal snigger his recognition of the preposterous nature of any such suggestion. 'God alive-o, matey. You're making jokes again. They all do that, matey. Come here and make jokes. Take it out of old Alf. Blimey-O'Reilly, matey . . .'

The sergeant had tugged Purbright's sleeve and was now addressing a quiet aside to him. The inspector nodded. He looked again at the garage proprietor.

'Three . . .'

Blossom's amusement abated.

'Favour number three,' said Purbright. He pointed to a packing case that had been pushed almost, but not quite, out of sight behind a steel cabinet. 'If you answer a couple of my questions without wasting any more time and then telephone Fen Street and report having innocently come into possession of four stolen car radio sets . . .'

'God alive-o, matey – how was I supposed . . .'

Love intervened with all the majesty of the opportunely observant.

'They were on that list I brought you last Monday, sir.'

What the police surgeon called his short-term autopsy report arrived by hand at Purbright's home a little after nine o'clock that evening. He scanned it and drove at once to Mr Chubb's house in Queen's Road.

The chief constable received him with a face that registered grave apprehension; out-of-hours calls always upset him.

'Potassium cyanide,' said the inspector, as if to put Mr Chubb at ease by tossing in the choicest morsel first.

'Good lord!'

'It had been quite cunningly administered, too. In the ordinary way, it is so lethal that the victim dies more or less on one's hands. Which, of course, could be very awkward, sir.'

Mr Chubb nodded, unhappily.

'But in this case,' Purbright continued, 'the dose had been put into a capsule which would take a while to dissolve. Traces of gelatine were still fairly obvious in the stomach. Grail was in the habit of taking similar capsules after meals for indigestion. Anyone could have emptied one – or more – and replaced the dose of harmless antacid powder with the cyanide. The two halves of a capsule slip apart and together again perfectly simply.'

'In that case,' said the chief constable, 'the deception could have been engineered at any time, could it not?'

'Oh, certainly it could, sir. The man carried a whole jar of the things. The exchange could have been made quite a while ago. The jar would thus have become a sort of unlucky dip.'

Mr Chubb frowned at the levity of the description, then looked narrowly at his inspector. 'Must have been a nasty surprise for his kidnappers,' he said. 'They'll carry a strong presumption of guilt, you know, Mr Purbright. Bound to.'

'Yes, sir.'

There was a pause.

'You sound a bit doubtful,' said Mr Chubb.

Purbright consulted the report. 'I made a special request for the listing of identifiable items of food. The pathologist has come up with these: "nut fragments, probably almond; rice grains; shreds of chicken; vegetable shoots". I'm sure you will find the combination very suggestive, sir.'

The chief constable managed to keep puzzlement out of his expression; he looked instead like a priest hearing confession of a heinous but interesting sin.

146

'It may be, of course,' Purbright went on, 'that kidnappers patronize Chinese restaurants like anybody else and even bring a snack back for their victims, but I think such an explanation in Grail's case would be pushing coincidence a bit far. You see, sir, his colleagues at the house last night obtained and ate just such a Chinese meal as would have included the items that Spenser found in Grail's stomach today. And we have learned that the order was specifically for four, not three, people.'

Mr Chubb considered for some moments while he unfolded a very white handkerchief. 'So you consider the kidnapping story to be just so much moonshine, do you, Mr Purbright?'

'I suppose you could put it like that, sir.'

'But what possible object could have been behind such an invention?' Chubb shrugged. 'Oh, yes – money – that's easy to assume –a spurious ransom demand – all that sort of thing. But the fellow's dead. That puts a different complexion on it. And I can't see what anyone had to gain.'

'Might there, perhaps,' Purbright suggested, 'have been quite distinct and independent motives at work, sir? I can think of two.'

With his handkerchief, the chief constable made a small, gracious gesture of invitation. 'Oh, yes, so can I, of course. But don't let me steal your thunder, Mr Purbright.'

'No, sir. Well, you have already named one of the possible motives – hope of gain. I understand that the *Sunday Herald* was prepared to shell out fifteen thousand pounds and keep the whole thing hushed up. A nice reward for a little ingenuity, cool heads and straight faces. I'm not sure, though, that I see a famous and extremely well-paid journalist in Grail's category taking the risks that must have been involved simply for his share of the money.'

'Yes, but he did enter the conspiracy – if that is what it was. For one thing, he helped to make that tape recording we heard. Or do you suggest he acted under duress?'

The inspector shook his head. 'Not really, sir. Although we can't altogether discount the possibility of the others having had to kill him because he refused to go through with the scheme.'

Mr Chubb gazed anxiously at Purbright. 'Is that what you think?'

'No, sir.' The inspector turned aside to where a cup of cocoa –

Mrs Chubb's kindly meant contribution to his survival of duty on a chilly evening – was cooling on a tray. He peeled back and discarded in the saucer the skin that had formed, then stirred the remainder thoughtfully.

'As I understand it, the story on which Grail and his friends were engaged proved to be much less sensational than they had expected. In fact, it was a dead duck. Faced with such a situation, it is quite conceivable that an egocentric and fairly ruthless writer might take drastic measures to protect his reputation.'

'Yes, but to invent a kidnapping . . .'

'It would not be the first case by any means of trying to hide a professional lapse behind some faked crime, sir.'

Mr Chubb continued to look unhappy. 'And the money motive, Mr Purbright?'

'One might look to the others for that, sir. Grail's status as columnist would have been of secondary concern to them. Which brings us' – Purbright resolutely attacked his cocoa at last and diminished it by half – 'to what, in Grail's world, would doubtless be called the mystery motive.'

'For the spurious kidnapping, you mean?'

'No, sir. For the genuine murder. And I'm sure we are going to find it the least obvious but most powerful of all. The least obvious, because it springs from a happening in the past that was not understood then and has been largely forgotten since.'

The chief constable's gaze had wandered to the clock on the mantelpiece. It was of black marble, fashioned in the likeness of a Greek temple, and had been presented to him on his completion of twenty-five years' chairmanship of the Flaxborough and District Tailwaggers' Society. He tried to think whether this was the night when the clock was due to be wound up.

'And the most powerful?' prompted Mr Chubb, suddenly aware that Purbright had paused and was awaiting his attention.

'Vengeance,' said the inspector.

Mr Chubb considered. He crossed the room to the clock, felt beneath it for the key, and very carefully prised open the glass cover. He inserted the long-stemmed key, which he began to turn only after having tested and taken the strain of the mainspring, while steadying the case with a bridge of long, finely-boned fingers. Had God not called him to the Colonial Office, Purbright reflected, Mr Chubb would have made a singularly adept safe-breaker.

'Not a very English attitude,' said the chief constable. 'But less squalid, of course, than money. You have someone in mind, I suppose?'

'Only tentatively, sir. But the field is narrow and inquiries are afoot that should reduce it even further. My main concern in the meantime is to guard against anyone else falling victim to this person.'

Mr Chubb looked at him sharply. 'Is that likely?'

'There are two candidates. I have set a man on watch over each, but that sort of thing is a luxury we can't afford for long.'

'Indeed, we can't, Mr Purbright. Let us hope our quarry breaks cover very soon.' The chief constable turned away to withdraw the clock key and gently, fastidiously, to close the glass.

A moment later, the clock began to strike ten. The inspector took his leave.

Chapter Eighteen

IT WAS ANOTHER HOUR BEFORE SERGEANT LOVE ARRIVED back in Flaxborough after what Purbright had told him encouragingly would be a nice visit to the seaside. He telephoned the inspector at once.

'No wonder we got no joy from the directories. The girl's mum had re-married and it was her *second* husband's name that got into our records – probably from the girl's marriage lines – registrars aren't always very fussy, apparently.'

Purbright frowned painfully. 'Sid, it is late, and I have had many tribulations today, including a goodnight chat with the chief constable. Let me just get clear what you have been saying in such cryptic terms. By directories, you mean the trade directories of Brocklestone-on-Sea . . .'

'For the late 1940s actually, yes. You remember there was no professional photographer listed with a name that tallied with what we thought was Edie Bush's maiden name. There was no Capper, in fact.'

'So we noticed.'

'That's because Mr Capper, who died a couple of years ago, wasn't her dad, but her step-father. Edie's real father died much earlier, of course, and he *was* a photographer. In partnership with someone called Clawson. They kept a shop on the Esplanade. Or studio, he would have called it. Very old-fashioned. Oh, and here's something interesting – the old beach photographer I was talking to remembers Edie when she and her brother were kids. Always dancing up and down the sands, the pair of them, he said . . .'

'The name, Sid. You can elaborate in the morning. All I want now is the name.'

There was a slight pause. Impatience always disconcerted Love, to whom it seemed a vastly unreasonable reaction.

'Well,' he said, huffily, 'it was the one you suggested in the first place. Naturally.'

'Don't go away.' Purbright rang off. He was at Fen Street in less than ten minutes.

Love was in the front office with the night duty sergeant. They were looking through a furniture catalogue that Love's young lady had left for his attention earlier in the day. Purbright disregarded this token of abiding sanguinity.

'Any word from Godfrey, sergeant?' Detective Constable Godfrey was the man assigned to keep observation on the home of Henry Pearce.

'Reported in at eleven o'clock sir. Said everything was quiet.'

'And Pook?'

'Not two minutes before you came in.' The sergeant drew towards him a loose-leaf message pad. 'He said three cars had come and gone between nine and half-ten. All bona-fide customers. Only one since then.'

'In the last half-hour or so.'

'Yes, sir. It *is* an all-night garage, sir.'

'Do I detect a subtle distinction, though, sergeant? Pook called the others "bona-fide customers". Was this last one in some other category?'

Pook's reputation as an officer notable for doggedness rather than intelligence was not disputed by the duty sergeant.

'Oh, I think Pookie was too over-awed to think about it much,' he said. 'He'd take the view that you couldn't get anything more bona-fide than a Rolls, whoever was in it.'

'A Rolls Royce?'

'Yes. Very splendid, by Pookie's reckoning. He was most impressed.'

'Get him for me, will you, sergeant.' Purbright sat and peered uncertainly at the station radio equipment. 'And I just want to ask questions – you do all the Roger-and-Out bits, will you?'

Soon the voice of Detective Pook was announcing his readiness to be of service. It sounded gravelly and conspiratorial, but voices do, Purbright reminded himself, when screened by coat collars in the doorways of shops.

'When did that Rolls arrive, Mr Pook?'

'Seven minutes ago, sir.'

'And the registration number?'

On Pook's promptly quoting it, Purbright looked with raised brows at Love. Love nodded emphatically in confirmation.

'Where's the driver?' Purbright asked the microphone.

'Talking to Alf Blossom at the moment, sir. I can just see them in a corner of the upstairs office. The car's inside the service bay. From the way he drove it in I'd say it's on the inspection ramp – that hydraulic lift thing.'

'Sergeant Love and I are coming over straight away. As you know, the man may offer Mr Blossom violence; if you see anything of that kind developing, you must act as the situation demands. I think it's unlikely, though, that he'll do anything drastic while his car is off the ground – he'll want to be able to drive away pretty promptly.'

On their way to the South Circuit, Love asked if Purbright did not find odd Pook's reference to the hydraulic lift.

'A car like that. It doesn't suddenly develop a fault underneath that needs looking at in the middle of the night.'

'Probably not, Sid. But how otherwise do you persuade a garage proprietor to let you bring it through to a part of his premises that's out of public view?'

Traffic had almost ceased on all but the main roads, but a few cars were still going past the South Circuit Garage, the facia board of which was lit in a garish pink. Purbright drove on to the forecourt and parked in the corner furthest from an illuminated, all-night, self-service pump.

A figure crossed the road and came to join them. It was Pook.

'They've left Blossom's office,' he said. 'They must be in the service bay, where the car is.'

'Is there no way of looking in?' the inspector asked.

'I've not been able to find one, sir. The entrance is through that main sliding door beyond the showroom, but they shut that as soon as the Rolls had gone through.'

'What about windows?'

'Round the other side,' Pook replied. 'Three. They're all filthy, though, and boxes and things have been piled up on the inside sills. That was all *I* could see, anyway.'

The slight emphasis on the *I* made acknowledgment of the inspector's notable advantage in height.

When they had picked their way through a sort of automobile boneyard, a peril-fraught clutter of parts of cars rotting in the rank grass of what once had been a meadow, they came to the back wall of the service bay. The three windows showed as dim, smokey-yellow rectangles.

Purbright peered in vain through the first two. The upper portion of the third appeared to be less obscured. With the aid of Pook's torch, he found a discarded oil drum. Love set it upright beside the third window and held it more or less steady while Purbright clambered up, selected a patch of glass that happened to be almost free of grime, and set an eye close to it.

He was surprised to find himself looking straight at the face of Mr Alfred Blossom.

It was not exactly a face in repose, despite the eyes being closed and the mouth slightly open. Rather did it express inert acceptance. The spectacles had gone; without them, Mr Blossom no longer resembled a pert mole. In the blue glare of the workshop lighting, the normally rosy cheeks hung like uncooked pastry.

Not only had Purbright to adjust to the change in the man's appearance; Mr Blossom's situation was even more disconcerting. He was propped in the front seat of the Rolls in an attitude of driving without due care and attention a vehicle whose wheels, by

Purbright's calculation, must have been four or five feet off the ground.

The last circumstance that the inspector noticed was, he realized, the most sinister of all. Blossom was wearing a cap. Not a cap, perhaps, but a sort of pad. Held in place on the top of his head by two chinstraps of adhesive tape.

And trailing down from the pad was a twisted string. No, not string.

'Bloody hell!'

Electric flex.

The inspector landed heavily between his aides. 'Quick, we've got to get in. He's going to try to blow poor Alf's nut off.'

They scrambled back the way they had come and looked up at the big corrugated steel door. Pook and the inspector seized its handle and levered themselves against it. They felt the dead resistance of an internal bolt or catch. There was no wicket door.

'We'll have to go over the top,' Pook said. Purbright glanced with some trepidation at the outlined edge of the roof, twenty feet above their heads, but Pook was already running along the forecourt.

'By the office stairs, I think he means,' Love reassured the inspector. They hastened after their guide.

Pook was waiting for them at the top of the staircase. The office door was by his hand. He ignored it. 'Along here, sir.'

From the platform on which they stood, a railed catwalk had been built above the showroom to an opening high in the wall dividing the showroom from the service bay. Seeing it, Purbright swallowed and took breath. Not as dreadful as that roof, anyway.

Pook cantered across like a goat. How brave, the inspector reflected, are the stupid. He took firmer grip of the handrail and walked forward, closely followed by Love, whose attention and admiration had been captured by one of the cars beneath them, a concoction of grilles and fins that Mr Blossom had accepted in settlement of a debt.

When Purbright emerged in the service bay, he found himself on a gallery that continued for about twenty feet along the side wall. At the end of the gallery, a flight of steps descended to floor level. Part of the gallery's width had been put to use as storage space; Purbright saw stacks of boxes, some small drums and canisters, and shapes in pressed steel that he took to be car body parts.

Pook was already halfway along the gallery, carefully avoiding the stacked obstacles as he advanced.

Purbright remained still for a moment and surveyed the scene below. It was dominated by the big car, held aloft by the scissored girders of the hoist. Blossom had slumped a little further down in his seat. His head now lolled forward, but his curious headgear was still in position.

At this distance, Purbright could not discern the wires, but he noticed that a battery and some tools lay on the floor a couple of yards from the base of the hoist.

Three other cars were in the bay, at various stages of dismemberment.

There was no sound. The only movement in Purbright's field of vision was that of Pook, now stealthily going down the staircase while he kept his eyes on a point beyond one of the cars under repair.

The inspector and Love hurried to the end of the gallery and began to descend. Their combined weight on the iron stairs put a violent end to silence. Pook, tip-toeing across the floor below, was so startled that he nearly fell into an inspection pit.

Simultaneously, there broke cover at the spot he had been watching a bent and stumbling figure, a man with a square-shaped load cradled in his arms.

It was Robert Becket, and he was carrying a car battery. He shambled with what speed he could towards the hoist.

Purbright shouted. Becket neither faltered nor looked aside.

Pook tried to interpose himself between Becket and his goal. He succeeded only in getting rammed by the heavy battery. By the time the policeman had regained his breath and balance, Becket was beneath the hoist and setting the battery down beside the one which, presumably, he had already tried and found flat.

'The wires, Sid!' Purbright shouted. 'Don't let him get hold of the wires.'

Love was only a few paces away from Becket now. He bore down, one arm held forward like a bowsprit.

Becket, crouched protectively over the battery, his back to the advancing sergeant, was holding the bared end of one wire. He gave it a turn around the nearer terminal post of the battery and sought with his free hand the other wire.

Love saw the outstretched fingers groping across the oil-blackened concrete floor. They encountered the wire, pulled it closer, grasped it firmly near the end. The freshly scraped copper core glinted as Becket picked it up.

At the same moment, Love made a homing plunge.

His left shoulder made extremely painful contact with part of the hydraulic hoist and his right ankle struck a carelessly placed can of grease, but most of the rest of him landed on Becket, whose upper torso was forced thereby into conformity with the unsympathetic contours of the two car batteries.

Purbright and Pook came up. The inspector watched Love rubbing his shoulder and his ankle by turns. He looked concerned. 'All right, Sid?' Love groaned. Pook helped him up.

Becket did not stir. Disregarding him for the moment, Purbright retrieved both wires, wound several feet together into a short skein, and tossed it over a projection on the hoist.

It was Love who assisted Becket to his feet and handed him a handkerchief to dab a gently bleeding wound in his cheek. 'Sorry,' said Love, who had done very little in the arresting line.

The inspector scrutinized the silent Becket. He looked ill and confused and very tired. No candidate for mad dashes to freedom.

'Take him to the car, Mr Pook. We'll be there shortly.'

To Love, Purbright said: 'How do we get this damn contrivance down again?' He leaned back to try and get a view of the elevated garage proprietor.

By happy coincidence, a partly recovered Mr Blossom had just pressed the button to lower the car's window. He thrust his head out and peered down blearily at Purbright and Love like a disturbed innkeeper.

'You jumped me, matey. What did you go and do that for? Who are you? I've not done anything to you, matey. God-alive-o. What did you want to hit me for? You didn't have to do that. Blimey-O'Reilly, I don't know what you're on about, matey.'

'We have not hit you, Mr Blossom. We are police officers. How do we get you down?'

The head rocked about drunkenly for some seconds, as

Blossom tried to break out of his bewilderment long enough to make sense of the question. Then he muttered: 'Lever ... red knob ...' and went back to sleep.

Chapter Nineteen

'HOW BEAUTIFULLY THINGS WERE MADE IN THOSE DAYS,' said the chief constable. He ran a finger along one edge of the hinged lid of a large boxwood case. The lid was open. On its inner surface was a label, yellowed by time and partly eroded by spilled chemicals. It bore a faded picture of an old-fashioned shop front, and the words, in ornate type, Clawson & Becket, Photographic Studio. There was a carrying handle on one side of the case. The inside was subdivided to accommodate photographic plates, filters and lenses, a number of jars and tins, and, in a compartment of its own, a small metal tray set on a handle.

'What is that thing's function?' asked the chief constable.

Purbright held it aloft in demonstration. 'It is the ancestor of the flash bulb. A small quantity of a mixture containing magnesium was tipped on this platform and fired off by striking a flint at the moment the photographer opened the shutter. A very violent reaction, I understand, sir – it could generate a welding temperature.'

Mr Chubb looked shocked. 'And you say that Becket ...' He left the sentence unfinished.

'... Clapped a flash-powder poultice on poor old Blossom? Yes, I'm afraid he did, sir. His intention was to use electric ignition, of course, not a flint.'

'Never mind the fine distinctions, Mr Purbright. His intention was monstrous, whatever the means employed. And think what a fearful fire might have been caused. All that petrol in the car's tank, to say nothing of what the man had deliberately poured over the upholstery. And the film, of course – your young sergeant told me Blossom was absolutely cocooned in it!'

'Becket's was an extraordinarily powerful obsession, sir. His attitude towards his sister was something we don't often see in this country – something almost Sicilian – was that how you described it to my sergeant?'

'I . . . might have done,' said Mr Chubb, who most certainly had not.

'Unfortunately for Blossom,' the inspector went on, 'Becket's fury led him into errors, despite his considerable intelligence and ability. He says in his statement, for instance, that he wanted to kill Blossom because it was he who had filmed the girl's performance. But Blossom had no skill at all with a camera – all his fellow members agree on that. The filming almost certainly was done by Pearce. I think he would have much enjoyed it.'

'Pearce comes out of the affair very badly,' asserted the chief constable. 'He seems to have given us no help at all.'

Purbright gave a slight shrug. 'He was a very frightened man – particularly when he learned of Henry Bush's murder. His first reaction was to ask if the person responsible had been caught.'

'Was he not aware that Becket was in the town at that moment?'

'Oh, no; he had no idea, sir. And until he heard that Bush had been killed, it probably had not occurred to Pearce that anyone outside the small circle responsible for making the film was aware of the involvement in it of Bush and his wife.'

'Did Pearce even know that she *had* a brother?'

'Yes, but he had never met him. Edith and Robert saw very little of each other after her marriage. Robert regarded Bush as a pimp – and I must say his opinion seems to have been borne out by events. After Bush left her and added insult to injury by setting the moral watchdog Grail on her, she wrote to her brother, begging him to help. He was a regularly commissioned contributor to the *Herald* and could have exerted a certain amount of influence.'

'And he refused?'

Purbright stared at Mr Chubb, whose patience with narrative was inclined as a rule to evaporate after a few minutes. He could recall very few instances indeed of the chief constable's having actually helped things along with an expression of curiosity.

'No, sir; there was no question of his refusing – he simply did not get the letter in time. He was abroad. Working for the *Herald*, ironically enough. By the time it was forwarded to him, his sister had committed suicide. As her letter hinted she might.'

It was Mr Chubb's turn to stare, which he did with considerable sternness. 'But the woman did not commit suicide, Mr Purbright.'

'I'm afraid she did, sir. Becket has kept the letter. He showed it to me.'

'Are you suggesting that a false verdict was recorded at the inquest?'

'An erroneous verdict, sir. And quite understandably, on the evidence. Most of which was circumstantial and, I might add, provided by Mr Pearce.'

Mr Chubb's expression of gravity deepened. 'I feel that that gentleman is going to have to answer for perjury.'

'You are, of course, speaking figuratively, sir,' said the inspector, comfortably. 'And I agree that a charge could not be sustained in court.'

'You think not?' The chief constable looked a little ruffled.

'Unless Pearce admits what I now think really happened – that when he found Edith Bush he had no doubt but that she had poisoned herself, and that he tried to expunge his own guilty feelings by rearranging matters a little so that it would appear that the cyanide deliberately spooned into her drink by Edith herself would appear to have spilled from a packet accidentally knocked over on an upper shelf.'

Gloomily, the chief constable pondered this hypothesis. What he felt to be unnecessary complications were beginning to spoil his earlier pleasure in the prospect of a neat piece of crime solving, fortuitously witnessed at close range by representatives of Fleet Street. Why did Purbright have to create confusion?

In seeming innocence, Purbright created a little more. 'Of course, you will be the first to point out, sir, that even if proceedings were taken against Pearce, no jury would convict in a case where the only crime would seem to have been an attempt to protect the reputation of a dead woman. The stigma of self-destruction is much disliked by respectable people.'

'And understandably so,' said the chief constable, who thought he had sniffed the sulphur of scepticism in Purbright's comment. He went on: 'It's a funny thing, you know, but a sort of old-fashioned chivalry has kept showing itself in this affair.' A slight shrug. 'In a perverse way, you understand.'

'Oh, yes,' agreed the inspector, at once. 'Becket has a distinctly quixotic element in his character. Which is just as well for Miss Clemenceaux, incidentally.'

Mr Chubb raised his brows. 'Really?'

'As you will see when you read it, he goes to great trouble in his statement to deny her complicity in any part of what was going on. In particular, he insists that she believed Grail's death to have had a natural cause; and that she had no hand in moving his body from the phone box where he collapsed to the railway station where it was found next morning.'

'Do *you* believe the girl to be as innocent as all that?'

Purbright considered, half smiling, then sighed. 'Birdie Clemenceaux is now back in London – if only to seek another job. So is Mr Lanching. So also is Sir Arthur Heckington and the *Sunday Herald*'s safely restored cash. Becket insists that the kidnapping fraud be laid to his account alone. The newspaper wants the whole business forgotten as quickly as possible. Even the mayor, I understand, is prepared to consider the town's honour restored. You must admit, sir, that an accurate apportionment of guilt and innocence would be extremely difficult to establish while so many people are being inspired to take chivalrous attitudes.'

Mr Chubb regarded Purbright in silence for several moments, thoughtfully at first, then with an air of increasing abstraction. 'Yes,' he said at last, quietly and slowly. 'Fine. Just you carry on, then, Mr Purbright.'

The inspector drove back to Fen Street from the chief constable's house in Queen's Road without encountering the usual confusion of traffic near the railway crossing and in Eastgate. He remembered the reason. It was market day once again, when this part of the town became relatively deserted.

As Purbright's car rounded Fen Street corner, it was saluted jauntily by Mr Kebble, on his way from a late lunch to a leisurely social session in the *Citizen*'s editorial chair. The inspector waved back.

Also bound for the *Citizen* office was Mr Hoole, visiting oculist. He had just left the Antique and Curio Centre of Mr Enoch Cartwright, whom he had given a cheque in payment for a pair of early nineteenth-century horse pistols, held on approval since the previous Friday.

Mr Hoole clearly felt he had secured a bargain, for he hummed as he strode on short legs across the Market Place and smiled a tight, shiny-skinned smile of recognition at a policeman in uniform who was stolidly patrolling the rows of stalls.

Constable Cowdrey did not acknowledge Mr Hoole's smile. Nor did he permit his eyes to meet those of one of the traders, a man who directed at him a challenging, contemptuous stare while he cut lengths of cloth for his customers.

Tucked behind his back, Constable Cowdrey's hands protectively enclosed a packet of sausages.

His limp was almost unnoticeable.